BEFORE THE CHAOS

A RIVAL HEARTS PREQUEL NOVELLA

MAGGIE RAWDON

Copyright © 2024 by Maggie Rawdon

Editing by Kat Wyeth – Editor (Kat's Literary Services)

All rights reserved.

No part of this book may be reproduced in any form or by any electronic or mechanical means, including information storage and retrieval systems, without written permission from the author, except for the use of brief quotations in a book review.

This is a work of fiction. Any names, characters, places or events are purely a work of imagination. Any resemblance to actual people, living or dead, actual events, or places is purely coincidental.

AUTHOR'S NOTE

Before the Chaos is the prequel novella to Rival Hearts, Madison & Quentin's full length novel.

1

Madison

WE'RE mid-game when there's a knock at the door, and we all look at each other confused.

"You end up ordering the pizza after all?" Xander gives my brother a look.

"No." Tobias frowns as he pushes back off the table and heads for the door. "Did you order something?" He looks back at me.

"Nope," I answer, shaking my head and frowning because I'm as puzzled as they are.

He pulls the door slightly ajar, peering out, and suddenly there's a loud greeting between him and someone else. The door falls the rest of the way open as the two men slap each other on the back. Shelby and Daniel, another guy from the team and his girlfriend, are just behind them.

"Quen!" Xander calls out in surprise to his and Tobias's other best friend and their college quarterback.

My brother and his two best friends Alexander "Xander" Xavier and Quentin Undergrove had been inseparable in college, but now that Xander and Tobias have been drafted and Quentin spent half his senior year benched, they're being forced down separate paths. Enough gossip and sharks circling that Xander and my brother had been pretty sure Quentin wasn't coming. Except he's here now and I'm not sure I'm prepared to be staying under the same roof as him *and* Xander.

My brother is best friends with two of the hottest men I've ever seen in my life. My crush on Xander has never really been a secret, but I've always managed to keep my thoughts on Quentin to myself. Because where Xander has always been a favorite of everyone in my family, only my brother has ever been a fan of Quentin. Mostly thanks to a family feud between Quentin's family, the Undergroves, and mine, the Westfields, that dates back to a collision on a football field two decades ago that abruptly ended my father's playing career.

My father's always bemoaned the fact that Tobias had to play on a team with him at the helm. And for his part, Quentin's played into the rumors—all tattoos, bad attitude, and general indifference toward anyone around him and sometimes seemingly even himself.

"Didn't expect you to come," Tobias says as Quentin steps inside and he greets Shelby and Daniel. Quentin's eyes fall over the room, moving to me as he sets his bag down. His brow rises and falls quickly—so fast you might miss it. I'm obviously an unexpected interloper.

"I needed the break. Thought it was just gonna be us. Didn't realize I was interrupting a family weekend." His eyes shift quickly away from me and back to Tobias.

"Oh, yeah, Madison came when we thought there'd be extra

space. She's doing her own thing while we're here. We can figure something out."

"Doesn't exactly look like a keg party." Quentin raises a brow as he looks toward the giant board game we have spread out on the table.

"We can deal you in. There's beer in the fridge." Xander smiles at his friend but I can feel the awkwardness building in the room.

"I can get one for you. IPA? Wheat? I think there's a local craft Tobias picked out," I offer, hopping out of my chair to head for the kitchen.

Quentin's eyes flash to me again, studying me for a moment. I feel my heart kick in my chest a little, worried that I've done something to offend him already. A half-hearted shrug follows in the wake of his assessment though and I can relax again.

"Whatever's fine."

"Okay." I nod, and round the kitchen island to grab a beer and the opener from the kitchen. "Shelby? Daniel?"

"Whatever you've got!" Daniel calls.

"Any seltzer?" Shelby smiles at me. I've met her a few times when I've gone to see Tobias, and she's always been sweet to me, so at least I'll have that.

There's more chatter between them all. Xander, Tobias, and Quentin exchange greetings and a general appraisal of the nightlife around here. So far, they've only found one bar they like that's open in the summer. We're up in the mountains of Colorado at our parents' house after all. A place that's really meant to be a seasonal ski retreat rather than a summer party house. So they've found more luck with beer and meeting women at the local grocers than anywhere else. Women that had already caught Xander's eye much to my chagrin. I'm pretty sure the checkout girl is ready to throw down with me over Xander, and she might win if I don't act fast.

I'M WALKING through the half-dark kitchen to grab a beer later that night when a voice startles me, sending my heart racing even harder when I realize who it is.

"You're trying too hard." His voice comes from the corner of the room and my eyes snap up to meet Quentin's.

"Too hard?" I go stock still.

"With Xander."

"I don't know what you're talking about."

"The outfit." Quentin takes the longneck bottle and sweeps it down to indicate the midriff top and extra short pair of shorts I have on. "The giggling. The bending over in front of him. Any of that ringing a bell?"

"I'm just wearing what was at the bottom of my suitcase. I need to do laundry." I lie. It was at the bottom of my suitcase but only because it was the first thing I threw in when I'd set off packing, knowing Xander would be here. "And I was just laughing. I'm not allowed to laugh?"

Quentin's shoulder rises and falls as he tilts his head and takes another sip of the beer he's holding.

"I'm just trying to help. Guys like me will bite for that sort of thing. Xander? His tastes are more refined."

I go through about five different shifts of emotions trying to make sense of that information. Whether or not Quentin Undergrove is hitting on me. The idea that Xander wouldn't find me attractive. The idea that I'm not refined. That Quentin thinks he can help with Xander—which isn't the worst idea now that I think about it. My brother would never, but Quentin might just be the right man for the job. Except first...

"Are you saying I'm not good enough for Xander?"

"Oh no. You're perfect. That upper-class thing you pull off so well most of the time. Just like your brother. I guess money does buy all that, doesn't it?"

He's in a mood tonight. I don't know if the trip out here was rough, or if he spent too much time in the car with Shelby and Daniel on the drive up from the Denver airport. He's set himself up here in the breakfast nook while the rest of us have been playing drinking games and cards, only occasionally coming around to sit in for a hand of something.

I'm guessing that it has something to do with the fact that Tobias and Xander were drafted and are headed for the pros, where he's courted injuries and the bench all season. His suspension this year had come as a shock to the college football world. A once promising career coming to a screeching halt in what had been widely seen as a series of self-destructive and senseless fuck ups. I mostly just felt sorry for him. I couldn't imagine what it must be like to watch your friends go on to get drafted while you wonder if you have a career left at all. Stuck in a no-win situation, trying to decide if he should go back to play college ball for another year in hopes he can make next year's draft or give up on that dream and try to find a new one. All while your friends get money, sponsorships, and women thrown at them.

Quentin isn't like Xander and Tobias. They both come from money—Tobias from our dad's money from playing pro football and coaching it and Xander's parents who are both from old money and deep pockets perpetuated by Senator Xavier's political career. They'd had private schools, coaches, and clinics from the time they could throw a ball. Quentin has gotten this far largely from pure talent. His meteoric rise to being one of the best QBs in college football and a forecasted top draft pick only to be stymied by bad habits and worse luck, has been rough to watch. The fact that his uncle, another pro coach like my father, has tried to help in the 11th hour and failed has only made the situation even more difficult for him.

"I'm just saying," he starts again. "He won't bite. For a million reasons including the fact your brother would kill him."

My heart sinks in my chest. I'd stupidly come to the mountain house to get one last shot at Xander before he goes to the pros, and I go off for my gap year abroad. One last chance at my longtime crush to get him to see me as something other than Tobias's little sister and maybe just maybe lose my V-card somewhere other than a hostel dorm. It was a long shot, and I knew it, but a girl can have dreams. At least until Quentin Undergrove crushes them with his ruthless honesty, but then I think misery just loves company sometimes. Not that I'm about to let it stop me.

2

uentin

"Oh shit. I didn't even think about sleeping arrangements." Tobias frowns as everyone starts to head to their rooms, and I grab the bag I abandoned earlier at the front door.

"I can sleep on a couch."

"No. Just let me think..." Tobias's brow furrows, and I feel guilty I came here all over again. He and Xander didn't expect me. Probably figured I'd be licking my wounds in private while the world burned down around me. But I couldn't take another minute of self-reflection or quiet solitude. I need my friends, some cold drinks, and maybe a one-night stand or two to make this all fade into the background for a bit. At least pretending for a while that everything isn't about to change for me. Walking in on a family weekend, and Daniel bringing his girlfriend isn't exactly what I had in mind.

"It's just... I took my room, Mads took hers, Xander took East's, and Shelby and Daniel took my parents' room. So we're full up. But I hate making you sleep on a couch. I could get you a room at the hotel down the way. It's the off-season 'cause it's a ski resort, so it might be a little empty, but you could just bunk there, spend the rest of your time here?"

I feel a lump in my throat at the idea of Tobias paying for my room or awkwardly begging to sleep on the couch to avoid any more time alone.

"He can sleep in the other bunk in my room." Madison chimes in as she walks by, avoiding looking at me and instead focusing on her brother.

"Oh yeah. I forgot about that." Tobias shrugs. "It's an option?" He gives me a hesitant look like he's sorry he's even suggesting it.

"I get top bunk." Madison adds and then finally looks at me. "And I don't know if you'll fit. But you're welcome to the bottom bunk if you want it." She sweeps some of her blonde hair behind her ear, and I try hard to stay focused on her face. Because my best friend's sister, who I only ever remember being an awkward shy nerd, has been transformed into a long-legged curvy goddess sometime between the last time I saw her and now. I almost didn't recognize her when I walked in—practically tripping over myself until I did the math and realized who she was.

"If you don't mind."

"Nope. Not a problem." She glances at her brother, and he just shrugs. I'm not sure if he trusts me that much, or if he's just that oblivious to the change in her. Because if she was my sister, I definitely wouldn't let someone like me anywhere near her—let alone sleep in the same room.

"Okay." I give a short nod and look back at Tobias.

"Works for you; works for me." He smiles. "I'm glad you came. Not the same without you."

That little admission from my old friend lifts a little weight off my shoulders.

"Well, can't let you run off to the pros without a proper send-off."

We say our goodnights and Tobias shows me where Madison's room is before he heads off to his own to sleep. I stop at the threshold and stare into the blur of girly frills that have been frozen in time. The walls are bubblegum pink and fairy lights decorate the edges of the bunk beds with fake ivy snaking up the sides of the windows. The beds are each made with a softer shade of pastel pink and frilly white with a row of flower-patterned pillows that line the wall. It looks like Barbie tried to decorate a cottage.

She's standing on the far side of the room brushing her hair, and she looks up. I must be making a face because her tone immediately becomes defensive.

"My mom decorated it when I was younger. I've told her it needs an update and bigger beds but she hasn't had a chance to get up here yet."

"I see." I'm short on words tonight and not eager to get myself in trouble. Because mention of her parents has the hairs going up on the back of my neck. Her father and my uncle *hate* each other. Pretending like the two of them don't exist is the way Tobias and I have stayed such good friends all these years.

"They're happy you're here by the way. The guys I mean. They were talking about how much they missed you before you got here. I know it's weird between you all now. I don't know all the details, but if you were wondering..." She talks a mile a minute, but the sentiment is there, and I feel both grateful and awkward in the wake of it.

"Thanks. It's a little weird, I guess." I run my hand over the back of my neck. I wasn't sure how to have this conversation with her. Really hate to have it with anyone.

"Sorry to be a bitch about the top bunk," she says when the silence drags on.

"I don't care about the bunk." Especially since the bottom bunk means I'm going to get an upfront view of her long legs every time she has to climb it.

"It's only for a little while. And it probably beats the couch. That thing is lumpy. I mean you're welcome to it if you want, but I figured this would be more comfortable."

"I appreciate it." I drop my bag next to the bed and sit down. The mattress sags a little under my weight. It was definitely designed for someone smaller than my six-foot-four frame but it'll do for the time being. Whatever I have to do to not be alone at some hotel Tobias paid for works for me.

When I look up, I see her unhooking her bra under her shirt, and I panic. The last thing I need is to see anything else about her I like. She's Tobias's sister, and she's clearly after Xander—those two facts are all I need to remind myself that everything about her is look, *don't touch.*

"What are you doing?"

"Taking my bra off?" She looks at me perplexed.

"If you're going to change in here, I should probably go."

"I'm doing it under my shirt." She does some sort of magic trick moving her arms in and out of her sleeves and then pulls the bra out of one of the armholes. The way she's looking at me, it's like I must be an idiot for not realizing this is a thing. But then, when women take their bras off in front of me, the tees are usually long gone.

"Sorry. Not used to… that." I feel like an awkward teenage boy right now. I'm not even sure how we got here in two quick minutes. This girl makes my head spin.

"Have to be able to change at camp or the gym or wherever." She shrugs but there's the slightest blush on her cheeks like I've made her feel awkward too, and now I feel like an asshole.

"Got it."

"You can change if you want. I won't look."

I try to stop the smile that comes from her genuine attempt to give me privacy. Like I might actually have decency and morals—worry about someone seeing more than they should of me.

"Yeah, when I'm at camp or the gym or whatever, we're all naked, so it doesn't matter."

"Okay well if you're going to get naked, that might be a problem."

"Oh yeah?" I shouldn't tease her, but the scandalized look on her face has me amused. "I think I'm safe given your interest in Xander."

Her eyes catch on mine and concern worries her face.

"Please don't say anything to him."

"Isn't the point of all that so he'll know you like him?"

"He already knows. Or knew. It was a long-running joke that I had a crush on him. But I don't know that he knows I still do, and I don't want to embarrass myself until I know if he's even remotely interested. I've always been Tobias's little sister to him, and I hate it."

"You keep up like tonight, I don't think I have to say anything for him to figure that one out." I raise a brow at her.

"So you think he's just not interested?"

Am I really discussing Xander's preferences with Tobias's little sister on my first night here? Is this my life now? Just a short while ago I'd have been neck deep in women of my own and now, I'm a relationship counselor for my wide receiver's little sister.

"He's kind of oblivious. But it's more like... Well, like you said, I doubt you register as anything other than Tobias's sister. I don't think it's that he isn't interested so much as he doesn't notice you at all."

"Wow."

And I've offended her in record time. I'm just tallying up a list of mistakes, and I'm guessing I'm going to end up on the couch soon anyway. She storms up the ladder, her long legs just as gorgeous as I imagined they would be up close, and I hear her bounce on the springs above my head in a huff.

"I don't exist because of a man I'm related to. Two hundred plus years and not much changes, apparently."

"What?"

"The Regency era. A woman's brother's behavior could decide her fate. Ridiculous that it still does. He chooses you as a friend, and suddenly I'm invisible. Men! Jane was right about so many things."

"Okay, well I don't know fuck-all about the Regency era or who Jane is, but Tobias would probably see red if Xander touched you. I doubt Xander thinks all that drama would be worth it."

"What would make it worth it?"

For Xander? I don't know. For me? I'm starting to wonder if there might be a price I'd be willing to pay.

"I don't know…"

"I just… I've always had this crush on him. It never goes away. He's so hot and so passionate about the things he cares about. I know with him going to the pros that I don't have a chance in hell of being a girlfriend or anything, but I was hoping I might at least get him to—"

She stops abruptly like she's realized she's talking to me and not one of her girlfriends. But I'm curious now what she wants from him. She doesn't strike me as the one-night stand type and that's the only way I can imagine that sentence going.

"Get him to?" I ask after the pause continues.

"Never mind."

"I mean there's only a couple of ways that sentence ends

and given the way you were bending over I assume you want him to fuck you."

"Something like that."

It surprises me when a flare of jealousy rises in the wake of her answer. I shouldn't even be thinking it. But there's something about the fact that she won't even give me a shot. That she's so sure I wouldn't even be a candidate, that she's content to be having a late-night sleepover chat with me on the bottom bunk—fucking stings like hell. At a time when most of my nerves are raw. I still feel for her though. What it's like to be up against terrible odds and hoping it'll still turn out in your favor.

"Well, good luck with that. Being Tobias's sister makes you practically invisible to him. It's not your fault. Anything you do or not do. He just has blinders in place."

"Ok. You're still not helping here. What would make me visible?"

"I didn't know I was supposed to be helping. I guess... Suddenly having a different family and name might help."

"I mean something practical..." she grumps.

"You'll be shocked to know I don't know the inner workings of what my friend finds fuckable."

"You've never paid attention to who he takes home?"

"Not really. Unless we're after the same girl."

"Okay. Well, see... you're not that different from him, if you go for the same girl sometimes. What would change your mind?"

"Oh little Westfield," I laugh. "You don't know me very well if you think me and the senator's son aren't that different."

"Little Westfield?" I hear the creak of the springs and suddenly her hair's draped over the edge and two blue-green eyes are glaring at me from above. "No."

"Goldilocks and the top bunk?" I tease her.

"Also no."

"Madison... Mads. Nah. That's not quite right. Madness?

Yeah, I think that fits if you're pursuing Xander." I laugh at my own joke but the blue-green eyes don't shift from their perturbed state.

"You're not being very helpful."

"Again... Why should I be?"

"I mean, I did share my bedroom with you. I could have left you on the lumpy couch. I feel like that should count for something."

"Bedroom, not bed, I feel like there's a different level of debt there."

"Yes, well you just made it clear the latter isn't an option." She disappears and another huff has her landing on the center of the bed again, the mattress dipping a little with the movement.

"Exactly," I say with more conviction than I feel.

"Okay. So what would change your mind?"

Just about anything right now. My nerves are shot to shit and I'm too tired to think straight. I could use a good fuck to distract me. And she's gorgeous and kind of sweet even if she does talk a fuck ton about Xander. Then again if she was too busy calling my name out it wouldn't matter. I run a hand over my face before I accidentally say something like that out loud.

"Did you fall asleep?"

"Madness." I laugh.

"Oh my god. That's a terrible nickname. It's not even very creative."

"No. That was my answer." Except after thinking for a minute, it makes sense as a nickname for her too. "But it's a great nickname too."

"Fine. Forget I asked. Goodnight." There's more movement, and the mattress squeaks and whooshes again before she settles. A moment later the fairy lights flicker off, and we're drenched in darkness.

I sigh. "I'm sorry. I don't know. I think it's probably a dealbreaker for him. Maybe if you were persistent. Kept up with the seduction thing but were a little more subtle about it."

"Subtle how?"

"I don't know. You're asking the wrong guy. Subtle's not my thing. Fuck it's not Xander's half the time either. But when it comes to women... you can't sell too hard with him. He's more into the girl-next-door type."

"That makes sense. I'm currently losing to the grocery checkout girl. But if I don't try, I don't think he'll notice me at all." There's a sadness to her voice, and I feel guilty for teasing her. I remember what it was like having crushes when I was younger. I'd been gangly, awkward, and usually dressed in whatever thrift store finds my mom could find for half-off with a haircut I got sitting on a plastic lawn chair in her boyfriend of the week's backyard. I know it hurts not to be noticed.

"You're hard not to notice." I say it before I can think through how it'll sound. I'm just trying to comfort her, and this isn't my strong suit. "The madness and all, I mean."

She's quiet for a beat, and I roll over onto my side when I think she might be done talking.

"So if I manage to tone it down while still getting his attention. Would being a virgin be a dealbreaker?" Her voice is barely above a whisper.

Oh. *Fuck.*

"It would definitely complicate things."

"For you or Xander?"

"For any guy with a conscience."

"Oh." Is all she says in return to that.

"Goodnight, Madness."

"Goodnight."

And I'm not sure I have a conscience given the direction my mind's already going. What it would be like to give her firsts. How that soft voice might sound moaning my name. What those gorgeous hips would feel like under my palms when I fucked her for the first time. I need to get a grip. I've fucked up enough things in my life. Fucking my best friend's little sister would only lead to worse things. That's assuming she could take her eyes off Xander long enough, which seems like it would be a challenge in and of itself.

Then again, I never did meet a challenge I didn't like.

3

Madison

As we make our way up the side of the mountain I try to pin back some of the hair that's fallen down into my face and hit my earbud in the process. It tumbles to the ground and I gasp, stopping abruptly to stare at the ground but tripping and nearly taking Quentin and I both out in the process.

"Whoa!" He grabs my hand as I slip on the incline and start to fall.

I desperately try to regain my footing and instead tumble face forward into his chest, knocking him backward. Luckily the man's like a wall and grabs the tree and then grips my hand tighter. A quick blur of motion, it stops us both dead in our tracks.

I'm embarrassed and my cheeks heat with it, extricating myself from the way I've tangled us. But a glance back down the side of the mountain we've climbed and I'm thankful he was there awkward or not. Otherwise I'd be a heap at the bottom, probably with a broken ankle or worse.

"You okay?" He looks me over like I might still be injured.

"Yes. I'm sorry. Are you?" I brave looking at him and his dark blue eyes are studying me curiously.

"Yeah. What's with the quick stop? A snake?" He looks down at the ground.

"A snake? What?" I tear my eyes away from him and start looking frantically around.

"No. I didn't see one. I'm asking if you did."

"No. I just lost my earbud when I was fixing my hair. I don't know where it fell to." I stop looking for snakes and start looking for the tiny expensive bud.

"Aren't we supposed to be communing with nature? What are you listening to?" He admonishes me but he helps me look on the ground.

"I was listening to a book."

"A book?"

"Yes. You've heard of them. I assume?"

He looks up at me, raising his brow as our eyes meet. "Smartass"

"Sometimes." I shrug in return, giving him half a smile before I return to sorting through the dead pine needles and leaves. If there is a snake, this is probably how I find it.

"Here," he announces before he leans over to pick up a small white bud out from under some leaves. He holds it out for me but when I go to take it he keeps it, holding it hostage. I look up at him and he smiles. "What book? Hemingway? Steinbeck?"

"No. We're on vacation. Not in English Lit 101."

"So what do you read on vacation?"

"Jane Austen."

"Is that the same Jane you were referring to last night?"

"You don't know who Jane Austen is?" I stare at him wide-eyed.

"If I don't, then what?" He looks at me like it's a challenge.

"Then I'm shocked. Haven't you been attending any of your classes? How do you get out of college not knowing that?"

"I've heard the name, Madness, I've just never read anything."

I skip over the fact that he's still using the ridiculous name he decided to call me because I'm too shocked he's never read Austen.

"Never? Not even in school?"

"No."

"Wow. She's usually assigned reading. I mean, she's worth reading anytime but I don't know how you made it out of school never reading her."

"I probably read the summary to pass a test. With practice and games, I don't have a lot of time to read old books. What does she write about?"

"What doesn't she write about? Society, struggles, politics, what it's like to be a woman, family dynamics, poverty, rising above your station, judgment and relationships, but most of all love."

He's staring at me like I've lost him, but he blinks at the last bit. "So love stories then?"

"Well yes, but it's much more complicated than that."

"Huh. That makes sense." Quentin starts walking again and I hurry behind him.

We've lost Shelby and Daniel at this point. They're far ahead of us on the trail but it loops around so we're bound to catch up with them on the way back to the car. I pick up my speed to try to keep up with Quentin who's way more in shape than I am—a definite advantage climbing uphill at this altitude.

"Why does that make sense?"

"You reading that makes sense."

"Why?"

"You just seem optimistic. Probably believe it all ends in fairytale weddings and happily ever afters, right?"

"I mean sure. I think they happen to some people. I hope good things happen to me. Is that wrong to hope for?"

"Nah. It makes sense is all."

"This another dig at me for having parents with money?"

"No. Just a dig at your optimism. But hey if you're lucky, you'll end up married to Xander, right? You can tell him you saved yourself for him. Wear the white dress."

"I don't want to save myself for him. After our conversation last night, I'd rather he not know at all."

Quentin turns his head back over his shoulder and gives me a skeptical look.

"Oh, he'll know."

"How?"

Quentin stops dead in his tracks.

"You've taken sex ed, right?"

"Yes, I've taken sex ed." I glare at him.

"You're aware you can bleed?"

"Sometimes but not always. I've done my research."

"Even if you don't. It'll be obvious you're not experienced."

"I can fake it. Fake it until you make it, right?"

Another skeptical look appears on his face and it irks me.

"He'll know. If you don't tell him and he figures it out—that *will* piss him off. Given how close he and Tobias are... If you take any advice from me, take that."

"If I tell him I'm inexperienced, he definitely won't want me."

"Exactly."

I bite my bottom lip to keep it from quivering. Getting laid for the first time is apparently a lot like getting your first job. Everyone wants experience before they'll give you a shot and no one but assholes want to give it to you. When Quentin doesn't hear me following him he stops and turns back.

"Come on. I don't want to lose you too."

"No. Go ahead."

Quentin sighs and walks back to me. "I'm just trying to be honest with you."

"Got it. Lose my virginity to some guy in a hostel dorm that I'll never see again."

"I didn't say that. I just... find a guy that's not Xander. At least at first. Experiment. Figure out what you want. What you like. Then come back around and try to have that experience with the guy you're obsessed with."

"I am not obsessed."

"Pining over. Crushing on. Whatever you want to call it."

I narrow my eyes at him, but I can't help thinking he might have a point. Doing this or at least some of this with someone else first would be less pressure. Less stress to get it all right if I could just be honest about where I am and the amount of experience I have—which is virtually none.

"Fine." I relent.

"Fine." He repeats. "Now stay with me. I don't want you getting attacked by a mountain lion or falling again. You heard the ranger. They've been spotted a lot around here lately."

"You," I say it with more confidence than I feel. He did say he was more likely to be interested than Xander though, so it's worth a shot.

"Me?" His brow furrows for a moment and then his face blanches. "No. No way." He turns and starts to walk away.

"I'm not saying you have to take my V-card. I just mean the chance to see if it seems like it's obvious that I'm inexperienced."

He gives me a sidelong glance before he walks off again. "No."

"So you'll just let me struggle along then. When you could help." I hurry after him.

"Why would I help you?" He calls behind him.

"I helped you!" I call after him.

"You already cashed that in when you asked for advice."

"You were grumpy when you got here. Flailing in the awkwardness really and pouting in a corner. Then panicking at the idea of Tobias sending you off to a hotel. I gave you an out. Help when you needed it. You could save me from the awkwardness too."

He stops in his tracks and puts his hand over his mouth for a moment before he turns to look at me. There's an accusation in his eyes. Annoyance that I'm bringing it up when we'd pretty much had a silent agreement. But we're alone in this forest right now and I don't see any reason to pretend it isn't this way. He relents. I see it change his face the moment he does.

"What exactly do you want me to do?" He asks reluctantly.

4

Quentin

"Just... try a few things with me. Give me your honest opinion. If I suck. If it's as obvious as you say it'll be."

Fuck do I want her to try things on me. She can use me however she wants. But I'm not going to be a good judge on this for her. Because whether or not she'll be good for Xander isn't something I'm going to be thinking about.

"I already know you don't have experience." I counter, trying to get her—and me—to see reason.

"Right. So you can't be mad." She grins at me. "And you won't judge me if it sucks. It's a good solution."

"Madison..." I sigh. "I'm still Tobias's friend."

"*Quentin*—again, do you want to be that guy? That treats me different because you know my brother? I don't think you do. Plus... just pretend I'm not."

"That's hard to do."

"Just imagine I'm some other woman."

"Again…"

"Oh please. Like you don't mess around with dozens of women. I'll just be one of them. It's fine."

"I actually don't."

It's her turn to show skepticism.

"I don't. I'm not your brother or Xander. I'm not saying I'm falling in love or boyfriend material. I've done my fair share of fucking around but I don't fuck like I have a quota to meet like Xander does." The last part isn't really fair to my friend but it comes out anyway. Probably because I don't like the idea of her hooking up with him. I'm trying to dissuade her from it if I'm honest.

"Maybe that's a good thing too." She shrugs.

"Good how?"

"Maybe you're actually good at it." Her eyes drift to my lips.

"And Xander isn't?"

"I don't know. Doesn't matter if I can't get him to the point he wants to try with me, does it?" Her voice is softer suddenly, a hint of huskiness to it as her eyes lift slowly to meet mine. "But you said you'd bite."

"If you weren't his—" I don't get to finish the sentence because her lips are on mine.

Whatever Madison misses in experience, she makes up for in enthusiasm. Kissing me like she wants me. Like I could just as easily be Xander. Her hands slip on to my shoulders and her fingers curl over them as her lips brush over mine. It's soft and tentative at first, seeking like she's just testing the water to see if she really wants to be doing this.

But she must, because a moment later it's deeper and I can taste whatever candy she'd been eating in the car on the way here mixed with her Chapstick—tropical like coconut and lime, and it makes me want more of her. So I do the stupid thing—I kiss her back.

I run my tongue over her lower lip and tangle it with hers, tasting her the same way she is me. Lost in the way her fingers play over my traps. I grab her and pull her closer. I let my hands run down her sides and over her hips, using my tongue to trace over hers. My heart is pounding in my chest and I can't remember the last time a kiss—just a kiss—felt like this.

When we break to catch our breath we don't move away from each other, both of us still dazed and me more than a little confused. I'm still caught off guard she'd kiss me like she wanted me.

"And?" she asks.

"And?" I repeat, staring at the way her lips are pink and a little swollen from the way she'd kissed me.

"Is it okay?"

Right. She was getting my opinion. That'd been the reason for the heroic effort.

"Yeah. It's not bad." I lift my shoulder, trying to keep my cool because in reality I want to kiss her again.

"Not bad? I thought it was pretty good. You're pretty good at it." She grins and her eyes are bright with amusement.

"I'm not the one being graded, Madness."

"You never know. You might benefit from some critical feedback yourself."

I raise my brow at her but she just smirks in return.

"I thought you wanted my help."

"I thought you weren't willing to give it."

"Maybe you just convinced me you need it. Desperately." I smirk back at her.

She punches my shoulder and raises her brow at me in threat.

"Ow!"

"If you're going to help me, you need to be nice about it."

"If you put my throwing arm out of commission I won't be helping anyone."

"Sorry." She has the decency to look remorseful and she rubs her fingers over the spot where she hit me. "Want me to kiss it better?" She gives me a wry grin.

"Yeah. Why don't you do that?" I challenge her.

She presses her lips gently to my shoulder through my shirt, but then her lashes lift and her gaze moves back to me. I slip my fingers under her chin and tilt her jaw back up to me, my thumb running over her lower lip before I kiss her again. She melts under it, like she's done proving something and instead just wants the taste of me because she likes it. Her fingers exploring again while I try to figure out how the hell this is so good.

We stay locked like that for several moments, me fighting every urge I have to let my hands wander lower or press her back up against a tree and pull her T-shirt off. Reminding myself that she's not in this for me and I probably shouldn't be enjoying this. But I want more of her. When the temptation gets too strong I pull away and her dazed expression makes it hard to hold her gaze.

"So you'll help?" she asks as she stands there watching me.

"I'll help." I agree, knowing full well I'm dooming myself because any taste of this girl just leaves me wanting more.

"Good. Then let's get back." She hurries down the trail ahead of me and I'm left wondering how I'm gonna keep up with her and keep this all on the tracks. Or if I even want to.

5

Madison

I'M SITTING with Quentin on the lower bunk watching TV in our room. Xander, Daniel, Shelby, and Tobias have gone out for the night and Quentin has stayed in, claiming he's still exhausted from the hike we took earlier today. I'm half-hoping it's because of me though. The way he'd kissed me in the woods certainly felt like it was about more than just letting me use him as a testing ground. The way he looked at me was like he saw something he liked. He and that kiss are all I've been able to think about today.

Tonight started as the two of us just deciding we couldn't fall asleep and him offering to watch some TV together. But now we're sitting on a bed together, almost touching, and I can't stop my mind from drifting to sex. We've been watching some sort of drama on TV that I picked based on about two seconds of the preview. A choice I regret when the second sex scene of the episode starts up and I have to fight the urge to jump up and claim I need a refill to get away from it. The tension in the room is thick. Like it has a life of its own and I can't take much more of it. If I'm thinking about sex, there's no way he isn't.

He finally breaks the silence and confirms my suspicions.

"Do you touch yourself?"

"What?" The word catches in my throat, and I nearly choke on the sip of the pop I've just taken when he does.

I feel the heat rising to my cheeks and panic starting to swell in my chest. I can't have conversations about touching myself with Quentin Undergrove. Him fucking away my V-card in the dark while I panic about whether or not I'm doing all the right things? Maybe. But anything beyond that seems impossible.

"It's fine if you do. Honestly, it's sexy as fuck if you do. You don't need to be embarrassed."

"I'm not embarrassed," I lie. "I just don't know why you're asking."

"Just asking to see where you are with all of this experience wise. How well you know what you like. Sex is more enjoyable if you get off doing it. Everyone needs something a little different to come. If you know your body well enough to tell him, or better yet to show him… It'll make it easier for him to do what you need." His eyes flash to the couple having oral sex on the screen and then back to me.

"I'm not having sex to get off."

He gives me an incredulous look. "Then why?"

"Because I want to get it out of the way before I go overseas and because I've always had a crush on him."

Quentin pinches the bridge of his nose and blinks.

"Get it out of the way for what purpose?"

"So I can have sex with whatever guy I want overseas without having to explain it's my first time."

"And then you'll worry about getting off?"

"I don't know. Do you think foreign guys are better than Americans?"

He laughs and shakes his head. "I think—as I said already—if you don't know how to get yourself off, you're not going to be able to help him get you there."

"Maybe he's just good enough to get me there. There are guys like that. Lana and Lo both said their first times were amazing. And Lana said she met a guy in Italy who could get her off barely touching her."

"Well... Then they're fucking lucky." He gives me a skeptical look.

"You would know? Because you've fucked that many virgins?"

"I would know because I have women who are friends who talk about their experiences."

I feel a surge of jealousy from nowhere at the thought of Quentin and his fan club discussing how easily they do or do not get off. I have no idea why. Quentin isn't known for being celibate, but I don't think he's quite the same as Xander. He wasn't lying about that from what I know.

"I bet they do." Is all I manage to say because envy would color any other words I might come up with and that wouldn't be fair to them. They're all probably way more sophisticated than me. Probably know all the perfect ways to give head and get a guy off. They probably have an actual chance with either Xander or Quentin. Maybe both of them—that's an overwhelming thought. I blush harder and bite the inside of my cheek to distract myself.

"Thoughts you want to share?" Quentin's studying my face, and he has a growing smirk.

"Not at all."

"So do you know how to get yourself off?"

"Oh my god... Quentin..."

"What? You asked for my help. I'm helping. I have to know where we're starting though."

"You're supposed to be helping me figure out how to get Xander off. I told you, I don't care if I do."

He only makes a doubtful face in response.

"What? Wouldn't that be more appealing to a guy anyway? Less work?"

"It's not work if everyone's enjoying it. So no, not really. I mean... maybe some guys, but I doubt Xander. Definitely not for me."

"Right. I'm sure that's your great love in life. Running around giving women orgasms. Not video games or getting drunk or whatever you get into on the weekends." I give him a look that tells him I don't believe him for a second.

"The two scenarios where I feel like I've made a fucking difference in this world are when I hit one of my guys in the end zone and when I watch a woman come for me."

I'm stunned silent for a second but recover, trying to deflect with a joke.

"Then I guess if football doesn't work out you can become a male escort?"

His face falters, and I feel awful for a moment forgetting his situation when I made the joke, but then he grins. "Why? You think I could get paid for teaching you the ropes?"

"I don't know. It sounds like you need a lot of instruction to be able to get a woman off based on all the questions you're asking. I doubt you'd make it long. Best leave it to the guys who can do it without the help."

"Now you're just baiting me." His long dark lashes lift and his deep blue eyes pierce through me as one corner of his mouth lifts in amusement.

"Not baiting. Just stating facts." I stand with smug amusement, planning to head to the kitchen when Quentin's hand wraps around my wrist, and he pulls me down into his lap.

My cheeks flush almost immediately because Quentin looks, feels, and smells like sex. That woodsy cologne that has a hint of citrus you can never put your finger on, the sheer size of him—at six foot four—that envelops me, and the way his eyes study me as mine fall to his lush lips. I don't know what I'm doing in his lap, but this close... all I can think about is how much I want to kiss him. How much I wish I was the kind of girl who could hold his attention.

"What are you doing?"

"Showing you what I mean."

"Meaning what?"

"Sit back in my lap."

I stiffly readjust, following his instructions but I'm trying not to let too many parts of our bodies touch. My heart flutters in my chest because for all my bravado I feel weak around him.

"Lean back and relax." He reaches forward and gently tugs my hair. It feels like he's inadvertently lit a match, my body lighting up just from that little touch. I try to do as he says, but I'm on edge. I don't know where this is going, and I always feel like I'm just one self-conscious bundle of nerves every time I'm around Quentin now. Xander is starting to feel like the easy part of all of this. Maybe that was the point.

"Madness, we've got all our clothes on, and I'm going to let you have all the control. Xander isn't here right now. There's nothing to be nervous about. I promise we take things at your pace."

I force myself to go soft, letting my shoulders and spine relax and letting my legs slip apart as I lean back against his chest. I can feel the rise and fall of his chest with each breath he takes, the exhale dancing over my shoulder and down my chest.

"There you go," he whispers against my ear, and I feel little sparks light down my spine from how soft and deep his voice is at this level. "Put your hands here." He takes my hands, the ones I'd just had balled up into fists, and places them palms down on my stomach. "Take a deep breath."

I do as he asks, and I can feel a little bit of the nerves dissipate. Breathing, even if it is in his lap is something I can focus on. Try to match my own to his.

"Take another and just imagine a place where you're not nervous. Wherever you feel most confident. That's where you are."

"Okay." I imagine the place he's telling me to. "I'm okay," I reassure him.

"Good." He brushes my hair off my shoulders and readjusts the position we're in.

I take another breath, and I feel his hands coast down the sides of my arms.

"Do you touch yourself?" he repeats his earlier question.

My heart skips beats in my chest, but I brave it out.

"Yes."

"Show me how."

I hesitate at first but then I slide my hands up over my rib cage and then over my breasts.

"You like to touch your breasts first?"

"Yes."

"Like this?" His hands follow mine and rest on the backs of them.

"Yes, like this." I show him even though I feel the heat rising on my cheeks.

"Do you play with your nipples?"

"Sometimes."

"Softly? Do you like them pinched?"

"Mostly soft. Sometimes I pinch. Sometimes I use my nails."

"Can I try?"

I don't know if I can handle Quentin touching me like that. I can barely handle sitting in his lap. But I think this might be a once-in-a-lifetime chance with him, so I'd better take it.

Besides, this isn't about him. This is about Xander. If I screw things up here, it doesn't matter. He isn't the goal. I could do this.

"Okay," I agree, and I slip my hands out from under his.

His palms cup the sides of my breasts and then work down, taking the weight of them on as my nipples start to peak. Even in the dull light it's obvious with no bra and me wearing this thin ribbed tank. One I purposefully wore to get his attention.

His. Not Xander's. I'd worn it knowing Xander wouldn't be here tonight. I'd done it for Quentin's benefit. When I admit that to myself my nerves resurface.

Quentin's fingers drift over my nipples, touching them softly through the fabric and then rolling them gently between his thumb and forefinger. The sensation is dulled by the cotton, but it still sends sparks of awareness coursing through me.

"Does that feel good?"

"Yes."

He continues playing with them, soft at first and then a little rougher before he repeats the pattern.

"Then what do you do?"

I slide my hands down over my stomach slowly, anxious even though I know I shouldn't be. Quentin is the *practice*. Xander is the main event. This is the warmup. If I can't be comfortable with a guy I don't care about, there's no way I can handle someone I've crushed on for years.

I feel Quentin's lips on me then, soft, and warm as he presses them to my shoulder. He dots a few kisses upwards, and I'm already imagining what it would be like to have him following my hands down my body.

"I take back what I said. You're good at this," I admit softly, glancing over at him. A small grin comes to his lips.

"You think so?"

I shrug one shoulder up, and he kisses it again just as my hand slides between my legs, and I use my middle finger to put pressure on my clit through my shorts. I close my eyes at the sensation. It's too much already. I'm already so wet from the conversation we've been having, from how wrong this all feels to take much.

"Is this how you normally do it? Over your clothes?"

"Sometimes... or at least at first."

"Do you have any toys?"

"No." I feel a blush come to my cheeks. "I did but then I was worried my roommate would find them."

I feel his grin touching my skin again, and he resumes the absent movement of his lips, kissing me in short little bursts.

"You just have to have a good hiding place."

"Maybe."

"Are you wet?"

"Yes."

There's a rumble from his chest but no audible response besides it. His eyes are glued to where my hand moves slowly between my thighs.

"Can you come like this?"

"Sometimes but not normally."

"What else do you usually need?"

The blush on my cheeks deepens because I don't want to admit the truth. Especially not to Quentin.

"There's nothing to be shy about, Madness. Everyone needs something different. That's why I'm asking."

"I usually take a bath. It lets me relax and the water helps..." I trail off. I don't feel like he needs more explicit detail than that.

"What do you like about it? The pressure?"

"Yes, but the warmth of it too."

"Have any of your boyfriends ever used their mouth on you?"

Just the thought of it has me imagining him, and the want I feel pools lower. But then I remember the one time I thought I was bravely seducing my high school boyfriend after my friend told me guys love doing it, and he outright rejected me.

"No. I asked Tom once if he wanted to try it, and he said he'd done it before with someone else and didn't like it."

"Tom's an idiot." Quentin kisses his way up my shoulder until he's at the crook of my neck and then he pulls back, his lips nearly brushing the lobe of my ear. "I'd do it for you if you want."

"I..." don't have words. I'm just imagining Quentin's face between my thighs. His tongue on my clit, and I'm ready to melt into oblivion.

"We don't have to. And it doesn't have to be now. I'm just offering if it's still something you want to try."

"Okay. Thanks," I say and immediately regret it, closing my eyes to try to forget how awkward and ridiculous I am. I'm probably nothing like the women he's used to. They're all probably confident and self-assured. They probably know everything he likes and doesn't.

6

uentin

I SHOULDN'T HAVE my hands all over my best friend's little sister. I definitely shouldn't be offering to be the first person to put my tongue on her sweet cunt. Especially not when her whole goal is getting my other best friend into bed. The senator's son who she actually wants. Not the friend with no pedigree, no money and soon probably no career either.

But Madison Westfield is in my head and under my skin. She's fucking gorgeous, smart, funny, and genuine—so fucking honest it's almost to a fault. So trusting that she's in my lap letting me play with her and confessing everything she likes. All while her brother could come home at any minute and murder me on the spot. Xander would probably happily help bury my body. Especially since his sister is about the same age.

I can't stop myself though. I'm fucking in lust with this girl. The way she laughs, the way she looks at me, the soft way she speaks to me when she's shy about whatever she's admitting to. The confident way she tells me off. That's before we get to how her brain works and the random shit that comes out of her mouth, or the way she knew I felt out of place when I first got here and offered me a bed to sleep in despite my grouchy ass mocking her attempts at getting Xander's attention.

I've always been more of a serial monogamist than anything. Where Xander and Tobias will have a different woman every couple of nights, I usually try to keep her around for a while. But a girl like Madison is more than that. She's the take-home-to-meet-the-parents girlfriend type. Except I don't have parents to meet or any idea how to treat a girlfriend. Which means I have no business even touching her. But fuck do I want to.

"Can I touch you?" The words slip out of my mouth before I can even stop them.

"Over my clothes?"

"Whatever makes you feel good."

Her hands go to the button and zipper on her jeans, and she undoes them before she reaches for my hand. She places hers on top of it and guides me the rest of the way over her abdomen, up over the elastic band of her panties, and settles my hand between her legs.

I have to close my eyes for a second when I feel the heat of her against my hand, count to ten, and remind myself this isn't one of the women I'm used to. She doesn't want me. Isn't trying to fuck me so she can say she slept with the quarterback or pretend that we mean more than we do. Madison isn't any of the things that normally give me anxiety. She just wants to experiment. She just wants to know how it feels and I'm only too willing to give it to her.

I take a deep breath and kiss the side of her neck, gently stroking my middle finger over her through the cotton. She's so wet, just that little bit of pressure has her soaking through, and I have to bite my tongue to keep from moaning.

There's a little intake of breath on her part when I pass over her again with more pressure on the next go. I watch her eyes close, and I kiss her just beneath her ear.

"I like the way you kiss," she whispers.

"I like the way you feel. The way you breathe when I touch you… you're gorgeous, Madison."

Her lashes flutter at the compliment, and she tries to sneak a look at my face when she thinks I'm not paying attention. At least until I pass over her again and she closes her eyes and rolls her hips up to meet me.

"Is this good, or you want something else?"

"Whatever you'd normally do."

I don't normally coach my friend's sister through her orgasm, so I'm lost at sea when it comes to this. Only knowing that I don't want to overwhelm her.

"There is no normal. It's whatever feels good for you. Whatever you think you want we can try."

"I want to feel your fingers on me without anything in between," she whispers.

I inch my fingers under the band a moment later, sliding them under the lace and cotton she has on, and there's a small gasp when the pads of my fingers slip over her clit. I groan when I feel how wet she is.

"Fuck, Madness. Are you always this wet?"

"Sometimes."

"You want my fingers inside or just over your clit?" I start to stroke her, and her eyes shutter again, soft sounds that are half moans and gasps come out of her. It's the most perfect kind of torture listening to her.

"Both. It feels so good. The guys before… Sorry. That's rude. It's just… You're so good at this. It actually feels really good. Like I could come just like this."

The praise she gives, knowing how earnest it is coming from her, sweeps over me. Leaving me wanting her even more than I thought I did before. More than I thought I could. This girl is like a riptide, pulling me under with every confession she makes.

"Has a guy made you come like this before?" I don't even know how I want her to answer. I hate the idea that she's been deprived, but I love the idea of being the first.

"No, not just like this. With a toy once. But he was pissed, and I felt guilty."

"Never feel guilty. Do you want a toy now? I don't mind if you want one. We can get you one for next time and try again."

"No. I want to try like this..." Her words break when she moans again, burying her face into me. "Oh fuck. That feels so good."

I smile at the way she curses until I feel her hand creeping its way up my thigh, coming dangerously close to my cock. Her nails dig into me through my clothes as I start to pick up my pace, her breathing gets heavier and her moans are a little louder.

"Shhh... Madness. You're gonna get us caught." I glance up at the door, half worried they'll come bursting through it any minute. We'll need every extra second we can get if they come home early.

"Sorry." She bites her lower lip.

"You're okay. It's hot as fuck. If we were staying somewhere alone, I'd beg for you to be louder."

Her eyes flash up to mine, lust written in them and it hits me square in the chest. She leans back then, kissing me softly at first, tentatively like she wants to make sure I don't mind. So I answer her with a rougher pass of my own lips, my tongue teasing along her lower one while I slide one finger inside her. Her breath catches, and she moans into my mouth when I slide the second in a moment later.

She's soaking my fingers, and her hips start to rock against the motion of my hand as I pick up my pace, her whole body desperate for me to give her the release she needs so badly. She pulls away, gasping for air, and tucks her head under my chin, breathing against my throat in a way that has me wishing I could feel it against my cock.

"Oh... It feels so good. You're so good, Quentin." Her fingers dig into me, and I feel her whole body quiver as she comes hard. It's one of the hottest experiences of my life, and I can't quite say why yet. Just that she's beautiful and sincere. So sweet and easy with the way she talks to me. A strange sort of pride swelling my chest that I gave her something she wanted.

She lifts her head then, a grin painted across her face and her lashes lower. The shyness that had been there before retreats a little in the wake of our joint victory. I smile back at her.

"Sorry if the kissing was too much. I know that wasn't a part of the deal. You just looked so... kissable?" She laughs.

"If that's what you like, I'm here for it." Her grin and her laugh are so infectious.

We both sit up, she rights her clothing, and I give her some space. A moment later though the silence has dragged on, and her lashes lift.

"Do you—is there something I can do for you?"

"I think we just take it slow. See how you feel about this, and if you want to try more tomorrow or something we can."

"You're sure?"

The look she gives me, I'd swear the girl wants me. Like if I gave her the go ahead, she might devour me whole. But I need to be careful with her. Pace this out and make sure none of it is rushed because the last thing I want is for her to regret it. Regret me. Because fuck if I don't suddenly care about how she feels about me.

"I'm sure. We've got our room every night for a while yet." I give her a playful smirk. "You should get some sleep."

"Okay well... Thank you for... that." I see the flush rise in her cheeks again as she gets up, moving to the ladder.

"Anytime, Madness."

She climbs it and soon after I hear the soft sounds of her breathing deeply as she drifts off. Meanwhile, I'm wide-awake staring into the dark abyss. My cock is still dulling from the ache I'm trying to ignore. But it's the ache that's moving north, through my chest that has me wondering if I can handle this.

7

Quentin

We're walking through town, working our way to the grocery store but stopping at half of the little mom-and-pop tourist shops on the way. She's currently licking her way through a chocolate gelato that has me grinning every time she gets a little on her chin in her exuberance.

"Listen. It's really freaking good. You need to try it." She holds it out for me, and I take it from her, taking a small lick and then handing it back.

"It's pretty damn good." Watching her was still better.

"Right?" She stops short in her tracks a moment later as we come up on a house in the center of the town, one I assume belonged to someone important a hundred years ago judging by the look of it. "Wow, this is gorgeous."

I follow her line of sight and nod. There's a for sale sign in the yard. It's beautiful. A perfectly manicured lawn, meticulously painted shutters and trim. A wrap-around porch with rocking chairs and planters on it. It's exactly the kind of home I was jealous of when I was younger and moved around with my mom from place to place. When my old man wouldn't pay child support and then when he couldn't because he was behind bars. I dreamt of a home like that one.

"I always wanted one like this." She's staring at it fondly. "With the cute little porch out front. And all the little rooms inside. One for a library. One for a sitting room. A fireplace. All cozy."

"You have a house like that... we're staying in it."

She shakes her head. "Not one that's my parents'. One that's mine. Theirs are never very cozy anyway. They hate older stuff—anything with character. It's always massive and modern with them. So big it almost feels empty even when we're all in it." Something in the tone of her voice tells me that growing up a Westfield might not always have been the dream I assumed it was.

"I always wanted a house like that too. Or at least I did growing up."

"Really?" Her eyes light.

"Yeah. There was one just like that we used to drive by a lot."

"What kind of house did you live in?"

"The back of an old Chevy." I let out a self-deprecating laugh. I have no idea why I'm telling her something I've barely told anyone. I'd rather they all believe I led the same kind of life they did.

"What?" Her brows knit together in confusion.

"My mom was kind of a wandering soul. We never stayed anywhere long when I was younger."

"Oh. You had a single mom?"

"Yeah. She and my dad split up when I was really young, and she never quite recovered from it, I guess."

"Oh. I'm sorry about that."

"It's okay. Probably would have been worse with them together, honestly. The few times they were in the same room together, they argued like hell."

"So did you stay with your grandparents or I mean, if she was wandering, how did you go to school?"

"Stayed with my grandparents some. Then with whoever her boyfriend was. I switched schools a lot until high school."

"Did she finally get remarried?"

"Not exactly. But yes, eventually."

"I'm sorry. I feel like I accidentally strayed into something you don't want to talk about. I didn't mean to."

"Nah. It's fine. It was a long time ago. She just dropped me off with my grandparents one day and didn't come back."

"Didn't come back?"

"Yep. She met a new guy. She liked him a lot, but he didn't want a kid around. He wanted the two of them to have kids together, and he thought I was an asshole. I guess I was a little bit."

"You were a kid. All kids are kind of assholes sometimes. They're figuring things out. Life is hard when you're little and can't make your own decisions."

"Well anyway… It was too much for my grandparents too. That's when my uncle took me in."

"Coach Undergrove?"

"The very one."

"My father hates him."

"So I've heard."

"He was furious when he found out you were going to be Tobias's quarterback. 'All that work. All those camps. And he's gonna have a fucking Undergrove kid tossing him fucking duds all over the field.'" She mocks her father's infamous voice. "I think he hated it more when he realized you were actually really good. Then when he found out you two were friends… I think he might have disowned Tobias if he hadn't been his only hope at the time. East was always a little more rebellious, and I think he wasn't sure if he'd play football or not."

"Yeah. Trust me. I heard about it from my uncle too. He thought I made the wrong decision in schools for a while."

"Well. I'm glad you didn't transfer. Are you going back this year?"

Another landmine question.

"I don't know. Hard to say."

"Don't you need to decide pretty quickly? I assume you need to be back on campus if you're going to get off the bench and play this year."

I cringe a little that she knows I've had so much trouble this year. I guess it probably would come up in conversation in their household. Probably another complaint from her father, this time about how we didn't make the playoffs because I fucked up and our backup was subpar. Hard to impress a girl who knows as much about football as she does when she knows you're warming a bench, and her father thinks your whole family is scum from an age-old grudge match. That's before we even get to the part where her crush, who's walking ahead of us a good stretch at this point, already has a starting pro contract. Might as well just squash any chance I have left while we're at it by telling her the soul-crushing truth.

"Yeah. I do. But I lost my scholarship. I might be able to manage a partial, but I can't afford school. My uncle's too pissed at me to pay for it after this last season. So I'm stuck figuring it out on my own."

"He won't pay? That's not fair. Not like he doesn't have the money."

"He has his own kids. I'm lucky he took me in at all."

"That's what families should do."

"Maybe. He's right though. I blew my chances. It's not his responsibility to fix it."

"Well, how much do you need? I'm sure it can't be that much. Especially if you can get the partial."

"Why, you gonna spot me, Madness?"

"Ha. I wish. My father's still pissed about the credit card debt I ran up last year. He was barely willing to let me go on this Europe trip, but I begged. Told him I can't take another semester of college until I figure out what I want to do. I was about to fail out on purpose just to have a way out. I just... can't figure out what it is I want to do."

"Yeah. Too bad you can't play football." I nudge her gently, and she smiles.

"But really... how much do you need? There has to be a way. It's a state college. Not like an Ivy or anything."

"Ouch." I give her a mock look of hurt.

"You know what I mean."

"It's still more than I've got, so it doesn't really matter."

"Tobias and Xander couldn't spot you?"

"No." It comes out harsher than I intend, and her eyes flash to mine. "Sorry, I just... I don't want charity or handouts. Especially from my friends. If I'm going to do it, I have to figure out a way to work for it on my own."

"And we've ruled out being a male escort?" I see from the way she smiles she can tell she hit a nerve and is trying to lighten the mood with a joke. "Because I think you'd be really good at that. Just a guess."

"I think I'm not cut out for that."

"Ah well... if our hands are tied that might make it harder. Underwear model maybe? A few nights of stripping?"

"Is this where your mind goes, Madness?"

"Just trying to think of ways to get you some quick cash." She grins. "Oh, what about a phone-sex operator? You'd be good at that too, I think."

I shake my head at her. "I think we need to be more practical. Maybe a checkout clerk. Or a part-time mechanic." I nod to the check out as we walk into the grocery store, and then nod again when I see the collection of car stuff tucked in one corner of the big box store.

"Those will take longer."

"But they're practical."

"When do you need the money by?"

"Last week." My smirk fades.

"Oh shit. Quentin…"

"There's a grace period. I have a few more weeks. I'm talking to my uncle when I get back. Might be able to write an I.O.U. or something that convinces him I'm worth one last bet."

"Good. You're too talented to quit now, just because there were some bumps in the road."

"Well, thanks, I guess. Sometimes talent doesn't matter in this world though. Especially if you fuck it up."

"So unfuck it. If anyone can, you can. We can brainstorm ideas tonight. You help me. I help you. We got this." She grins at me, and I almost feel like I could believe her. That a late-night, slumber-party style brainstorming session between the fairy lights and the frilly pink pillows could save my career.

We've wandered through the aisles, and she comes up short when we get to the end of this one. Her eyes fall on something in front of us again, and I follow. This time it isn't a cozy house though. It's a brunette woman who flips her hair over her shoulder as her eyes rake up all six-foot-five inches of Xander.

"She's winning this, isn't she?" I see a look of defeat on Madison's face, and I want to kiss it away. But Tobias is somewhere in this grocery store, and I'd rather not die between the frozen peas and pizza.

"Not yet," I argue, even though I don't want to. I want her to give up on him and look at me like she did last night again.

"She's so pretty. I can't even really be mad. I just want to ask her for makeup tips and what shampoo she uses." Madison sighs.

"She's not prettier than you."

Madison gives me a flat look, and her eyes dodge back and forth between the other woman and herself. The other woman is a few years older than Madison, and she also clearly spends time in the gym to make sure her legs and ass look great in the shorts she's wearing. But Madison is every bit as beautiful and then some. She just doesn't quite have the confidence yet to pull off her own skin. Once she does, she'll be an absolute man-eater, and I pity any man who crosses her path.

"That's why he can't keep his eyes off her."

"She's... uncomplicated." I shrug. "You're incredibly complicated. That tilts the scales out of your favor in a way that's hard to make them even again. But it's not because she's better than you."

"Complicated how? Because of Tobias?"

"That's part of it."

She gives me an irritated look, like she doesn't quite believe me and thinks I'm making up excuses to dull the blow to her feelings.

"Well... I like a challenge." She grabs my forearm and hurries me toward another aisle. And when we arrive, I nearly choke.

"Madness, I'm not about to be caught perusing condom options with you. If Tobias comes up here..."

"So be quick. What kind do I need? And do I need to get lube?" She grabs some off a shelf and holds it up. Images of the two of us are flashing through my head and I'm desperately trying to recover.

"Uh... It doesn't hurt. If you think you want it."

She chucks it into her basket and then points at the condoms.

"Okay, this is where I always get incredibly confused. All these brands and ribs and sizes. What size do you think he is?"

"Jesus. Okay... I'm sure he has his own. And please don't ask me to tell you what size dick my friend has, okay?" I start to walk away.

"Well, what size are you? I'm sure it's similar. You're only a little smaller than him." She finally looks up at me, and my face must be saying something because she suddenly looks remorseful. "I mean I didn't mean that you were smaller than him. I'm sure you're big. Huge even. Bigger than him I just meant height-wise, you know?"

I scrub a hand over my face and try to remember she means well.

"I think we're done here." I turn to walk down the aisle.

"Wait though. Do you have a favorite kind?"

I look back at her. "Why?"

She shrugs and gives me a sheepish look, and then turns back to look at them. "I just—I need to know what kind to buy. I mean, to take with me to Europe."

I raise a brow at her and point to the kind I usually use. "Those."

She grabs them and tosses them in her basket alongside the ice cream, pop, and other snacks she's picked up along the way.

"All right." She hurries to catch up with me as I walk fast to get out of the aisle. "Aren't you getting anything?"

"Nah. We're going out tonight. I'll get something then."

"You are? Oh." She looks a little sad at that, and I feel bad that she's too young to go with us. I'm tempted to stay home with her again but I know I need distance from her, not to mention Tobias and Xander will get suspicious.

"Look at the bright side, means he won't be at the grocery store."

She makes a face. "Assuming that wasn't what he was asking her just now."

"Well, I'll try to run some interference for you if we run into her at the bars."

"So you can take her home?" She studies my face.

"If she goes with me, she can't go with him, right?" I don't mean it. She's not my type and after just that little taste of Madison, I can only imagine everyone else will pale in comparison. I'm just saying it to test her reaction.

"I guess. Where are you going to take her? Not like there's anywhere at our place."

"You didn't have roommates fuck in the bed next to yours in college?"

"Uh. No. My roommate this year was even quieter than I am. I don't think she's ever looked at a boy, or even let one see her ankles."

"Her ankles?" I raise a brow as we hit the self-checkout line. I glance up, thankful that Tobias isn't here to see what she's buying and that I've been meandering around the store with her. I've rarely seen Tobias get pissed off, and I'd like to keep it that way.

"Never mind." She laughs. "Inside joke."

8

Madison

I GLANCE at the time on my phone. I haven't been able to sleep. It's almost two. All the guys and Shelby are still out, and I'm alone in this place—still too young to hit any of the bars they were planning to go to. At least when I go on my gap year trip I'll be able to go out. I can drink and get in to all the clubs and bars. I won't be stuck home alone wishing I could be out.

I'm not sure it'd make much of a difference to how the night ends but at least I wouldn't be sitting here wondering. I sigh and flip back to the website I was looking at on my phone.

It's the real estate listing for the house Quentin and I saw today. It's even prettier on the inside, perfectly kept by someone who has tastes similar to mine. I've been daydreaming about what it'll be like to have my own money and have a house like this someday. Something that fits my tastes. A home I can make all my own. One that actually feels warm and cozy.

This place would be perfect for it. But I definitely can't afford it now. Would never be able to afford it without a good job—if I ever figure out what I want to do for a living. I'm half-stuck in the daydream when I hear laughter burst through the front door in the distance and loud male voices that eventually disperse down the hall to bedrooms.

My heart skips when my door doesn't open. If he went home with someone, I doubt he'd bring her back here. So if he didn't come back with the rest of the guys, it means he's probably not coming back tonight at all. My time with Quentin might be up before it's barely started.

I wait another couple of minutes, but I don't hear anything and my heart bottoms out. It takes me a full minute to remember I'm not even supposed to care about Quentin. This is all supposed to be about Xander. He's the one I was after—the one I was trying to get into bed—that I've had this ages-old crush on. But all I can think about is Quentin. Quentin's eyes. His hands. His tattoos. The way he smiles at me. How he sees me in a way no one really has. How he treats me like an equal and not some half-pint sidekick of my brother's.

I should have said something today. Should have told him that he's the only one I want. But I was too nervous. Because with Xander, nothing's really on the line. My crush on him isn't exactly a secret to anyone, including Tobias, and because as much as I might crush on him, the way he treats me like a kid has made it pretty clear there's no chance. But with Quentin—it felt real. Even if it wasn't.

A flash of him with some other woman has my heart in my stomach again, and now I need something to numb the pain. I climb down the ladder of the bed and put a T-shirt and shorts on. I thought I was so clever waiting for him in my bra and panties like some kind of seductress, and now I feel foolish. At least I thought to buy some ice cream when I'd ambitiously bought condoms.

I check to make sure the coast is clear when I head for the kitchen, but all the lights are off and the only voices I hear are muffled behind closed doors. So I hurry down the hall and across the living room, quietly pulling out a bowl and spoon before I grab the ice cream out of the freezer. I heap one large scoop first and then another for good measure because fuck it, my heart needs the comfort right now. Then I slide the container back into the freezer.

But when I turn to head back to my room, I hear a noise from the deck, and I notice the door is ajar. The screen slider's pulled across, and the glass is pulled back like someone's stepped outside.

"Hello?" I call.

I hear another sound. A little like a crash and then silence.

"Who's out there?" I try to lean forward to see, but there's not enough light from this angle.

I hear another sound, like someone sitting in one of the chairs out there, and now I know someone's fucking around. I'm half worried it's an intruder. I'm pretty sure if this is a horror movie, this is how I die. Heartbroken with my ice cream in the middle of the night. At least it'll buy Tobias and Xander time to escape.

I pull the screen back and step out into the night. The air is a little chilly, and my eyes have to adjust to the moonlight, but then I see Quentin, sprawled out on one of the deck chairs next to the hot tub, a bottle of water in hand and two more on the side table next to him. He looks at me like a deer in headlights.

"What are you doing?" For once I get to raise my eyebrow at him.

"Sobering up." He looks guilty as he holds up the bottle of water.

"And outside on the deck in the middle of the night is the best place for that?" It's an odd place to be but at least he's here and alone.

"It seemed like it." He shrugs, amusement dancing over his face.

I make my way over to him and sit on the deck chair next to his. Apparently I was going to have to counsel the drunk guy out of the stupid idea.

"I don't think that's a great idea. They said there have been bears and mountain lions around here in the last couple of weeks. Remember?" I glance out into the woods that the property backs up to.

"Which is why I didn't have food..." He eyes my ice cream bowl. "Midnight snack?"

"Maybe."

"Is it the same kind you had before?"

"No. This is cookie dough."

"Oh fuck. I love cookie dough."

I hold out a spoonful and he leans forward and takes the bite off the spoon, swiping at his lip where some of it lingers and my eyes are drawn to his mouth.

"Fuck that's good. Ice cream is my weakness. You can't keep having it around all the time."

"Oh yeah?"

"Yeah." His eyes drift over me for a moment before he blinks. "You should go back inside. It's not safe out here. You said so yourself."

"I'm not going in until you do."

"Madness..." He drags a hand over his mouth as he watches me eat another bite.

"What?"

"I need to sleep out here."

"Why?"

"Because I've had too much to drink."

"We covered that. You've got water, and you're going to sleep it off." I scoot from my deck chair to his, and he moves slightly so we both fit. I hold out another bite of ice cream and he takes it.

"Yeah. Out here."

"You have a bed, inside," I argue and feed him another bite.

"I've been drinking. You're in there and..." he trails off and looks out toward the woods behind the house. I wait for him to finish, stuffing another bite of ice cream in my own mouth to try not to sound too desperate. But when he doesn't answer I can't handle the silence.

"And what?" My heart skips a beat.

"And just sitting here with you, eating ice cream has me thinking fucked up thoughts."

"Like what?" I turn and boost myself up, moving one leg over to the other side of his thighs and offering him more.

That's the other thing about Quentin. The way he looks at me. The way he talks to me. It makes me feel brave in a way I've never felt with another guy.

He takes the bite and groans as I shift in his lap. I can feel him going hard beneath me, and the heat of that knowledge rises up my neck and stains my cheeks. But I rock over his lap, anyway, testing his resolve.

His hands go to my ass, stilling my movement, and his eyes darken, a warning in them that I'm pushing limits he doesn't think I should. But I just grin in return and eat the last bite of ice cream. I set aside the bowl and turn back to him.

"Like what?" I ask again.

"Like how much I want to taste you."

"So taste me." I lean forward and kiss him tentatively. He returns it, and his hands dig into my ass as his kiss turns rougher, one of them pulling away and drifting up my arm and shoulder until his fingers slip around the back of my neck. He tilts my chin up and kisses his way down my throat. He's slow about it, like he's taking his time. Like he wants *me*. And I've never felt sexier than I do right now.

"I love the way you kiss, but that's not the taste I want..." He breathes against my skin, and I can practically feel the tension radiating through his body.

"You can have that too. I want it—so badly. It's all I can think about since you mentioned it," I whisper.

"Fuck me..." he groans against my shoulder, but his hand slips under the T-shirt I have on, and his fingers splay over my skin.

"I was waiting for you tonight," I say, trying to summon the bravery I wish I had earlier.

"What?" His brows knit together, and he looks up at me.

I shrug. "I thought... I don't know what I thought. I was waiting for you half-undressed though. Almost climbed in your bunk."

"Madness, fuck... You can't tell me stuff like that. It's why I came out here and stayed away from you."

"You don't want me?" My bravery falters.

"I want you—fuck do I want you. But—" I put my fingers over his lips, and then lean in to kiss my way up his neck. His palms slide over me again and his fingers dig in like he doesn't want to let me go.

"Then taste me. *Please*. I need it."

He breaks. I can see it on his face, the moment he decides to say fuck it, and have his cake and eat it too. His grip on my ass tightens, and before I know what's happening, I'm lifted into the air and he switches our positions, placing me in the lounge chair.

I slip my shorts off as he kneels down in front of me. His hands slide under the waistband of my panties, tugging them down my thighs and dragging them over my calves until he tosses them on top of my shorts. He kisses the inside of my ankle and then another on the inside of my leg, slow torturous drags of his lips and tongue as he makes his way up.

He kisses the top of my thigh and then his eyes raise to meet mine. My heart is in my throat, and I'm so turned on by being in this position with him I don't know that it'll take more than a few touches from him for me to be falling apart in his hands.

"Are you sure?"

More sure than I've ever been in my life.

I nod. "Very."

"Sit forward and spread for me then." He curls his fingers toward himself and I do as he asks.

"This good?" I ask, still nervous despite how much I want this and hoping I don't do anything wrong.

"So fucking good." His eyes are caught between my thighs, and his hands press to spread me a little wider. "You have such a pretty fucking pussy." I see his throat bob as he swallows.

He spreads me and leans forward, his tongue taking a long drag, and I have to bite my cheek to keep from crying out, half a whimper escaping instead. The warmth of his mouth. The way my nerve endings light up under the touch of his tongue. I can barely take it.

He follows suit with another round, and my fingers wrap around the arms of the wooden chair. He was right about Tom being an idiot, but I'm also thankful I'm getting Quentin for this instead of him. All my bad luck with guys finally paying off with someone profoundly good.

But the next bit, where he teases my clit over and over with the tip of his tongue and then sucks has me gasping. Every time my mind threatens to slip to some nervous or self-conscious place he drags my attention back to him. Keeping me focused on how good he feels.

It's like I'm being tortured and having the most exquisite sort of pleasure I've ever had in my life. I reach out and my fingers twist through his hair as he works me over. He takes one of my legs, lifting it over his shoulder, and I lean back further in the chair. I spread wider for him, and he devours me like I'm the best thing he's ever had.

When he slips two fingers inside of me, moving in and out to the same rhythm of his mouth, I feel like I might just die here. It would be fine. A beautiful place to die really.

I lean back further and look up at the sky as he pauses to kiss the inside of my thigh. It's so dark out here even with the moon, and all of the stars have it lit up, glittering like tiny diamonds against the inky-blue sky. I only have a moment to appreciate though before he takes me with his mouth again.

He starts to suck on my clit once more, and I can't help the moan that comes out next, one where I beg him to give me more and cry out about how I can't take it in intervals. He's rougher with me than he has been in the past, like he's not as worried that I'm glass that will shatter, and maybe, I hope, chasing something he wants as much as I do.

A few moments later my body can't take anymore. I break on the next wave, and it blooms into the kind of orgasm that has my legs shaking and me gasping for my next breath. The kind that I've never really had before, even after I thought the other night was as good as I could hope for. He kisses me gently through the last of it, his fingers slipping out of me slowly, and his kisses grow more languid as he works his way back down my thighs.

The warmth that's spread through every limb of my body starts its inevitable retreat and I start to sit up. He sits back on his heels and kisses my knee, grinning as he looks up at me.

"And?" he asks.

"You're good at everything. As usual." I smile back at him.

"Madness, I—" he starts but there's a noise in the woods, and it distracts us both. One that sounds like something large made it. I put my hand on his shoulder, and he runs his down the back of my calf. "We better get inside."

"Yeah..." He grabs my panties and helps me slip back into them, and I grab my shorts and throw them on too. The only thing worse than getting eaten by a mountain lion is walking in half naked to an audience of my brother and his friends.

9

Quentin

THE FEAR of getting killed on a deck after having the best fucking time of my life has sobered me just enough when I get inside that I grab another water and head to her room quicker than I should. Madison's hurrying along just behind me, and she shuts the door, leaning against it laughing softly.

"That would have been an awkward way to die."

I grin back at her and down the water. I can still taste her on my tongue, and fuck if I don't want more of her. Anything she'll give me. Especially when she looks at me like she did out there. Like I'm her own personal god, and she'd do anything for me. But it still surprises me when a moment later she reaches for my belt.

"Madness..." I say, half-warning and half-questioning.

"Quentin..." She mocks my tone.

"What are you doing?"

"Returning the favor."

My hand's at her wrist a second later, stopping her in her tracks. I shake my head.

"No. This was about you getting to experience that and what it felt like. For you. Not me."

"What if this is about me too?"

I give her the same flat look she's given me in the past.

"I'm serious. I want to. But you haven't let me touch you so far. Is there something... do you not think I can or—" She falters and looks up at me. "Oh. I didn't... Do you not get hard enough—I mean, are you not attracted to me enough?" The doubt that colors her tone tears a hole into my resolve.

"I don't know if I've ever been as attracted to anyone as I am to you, Madness." It's too much. Too honest because between the alcohol I've had and being drunk on the taste of her, I can't censor myself like I should. Her lashes flutter and then a small grin forms.

"Then let me do this for you. Please?"

I'm fucked because I can't say no to her. I'm trying and the word is failing to make it past my throat. I want her more than I've wanted anything in my life right now.

"Yes. Fuck... Okay. Yes but go slow. If you hate it or something, just say so. Okay? I don't want you to feel like you have to." Now I'm nervous, because if she hates this I'm going to feel like an asshole. Not to mention it's going to hurt and I'm going to have to bury that reaction fast. I take a breath and run my palms over her forearms.

Her fingers tug at my belt and I help her undo it and my pants and boxers. I sit down on the lower bunk and she hits her knees in front of me. Her eyes fall to my cock and I see the way they go wide. Her tongue teases over her lower lip and I can't fucking wait to know what it feels like. She hesitates before she touches me though, her hand hovering just over my cock.

"I'm so nervous though. I don't want to hurt you or like... be bad at this." She looks up at me. "I'm sorry. That's not sexy. I just..."

"You don't have to do this." I slip my hand around hers and press her palm against the mattress.

"No. I mean, I want to. I really want to. I just don't want to fuck it up."

"You won't be bad. I promise this is hard to fuck up. Just go slow and ask questions if you want. Like with all of this. If you're not sure. Just ask."

"Asking feels... not sexy."

I smile at her and slip my fingers under her chin. "Don't worry about not being sexy. Everything you do is sexy. You yell at me about the Regency era, it's sexy. You stomp up this ladder pissed at me, it's sexy. You eat ice cream and it's fucking sexy. I promise you're good."

She smiles back, and her eyes light with renewed confidence.

"Okay." I hear the resolve in her tone.

Her eyes fall back over me and her fingers wrap tentatively around me. She tightens them just a bit and then starts to stroke my cock gently. Just her touch feels like it could be enough. Enough that it's heightening the need I already have, making me harder, and I close my eyes to focus on it. I'm lost in it, just the feel of her palm over my skin and the careful way she works me over has me leaning back on the bed, bracing myself. I'm not even sure I need her mouth.

At least not until I feel the warmth of her tongue circle the tip of my cock. Her lips wrap around me a second later and I nearly jolt at how fucking good it feels. I will myself to stay still though. I want her to have full control over this experience. Do everything I can to make it a good first time for her because she deserves it.

I slide my lids open slowly. I know the sight of her doing this will be too fucking good to take, and I'm right. Watching her mouth bob over my cock, the way she makes it glisten, and how focused she is on getting it right, small lines forming on her brow as she concentrates.

"Look at me," I whisper.

Her lashes lift a moment later and her blue-green eyes take me in. She must like what she sees on my face because I see it reflected in her. The kind of joy you can only feel when you know you've got someone wrapped around your finger, on the edge of their sanity because the pleasure you're giving them is the only thing they can focus on. The way I'd felt outside.

"Feels so fucking good I can barely stand it. You're doing so good."

She thanks me by running her tongue underneath and around, picking up her pace just a bit more than she was before and I have to curl my fingers around the mattress to keep myself from touching her. She keeps it up for another few seconds before she pulls away.

"What do you need to come?"

"Just more of that. Your tongue. Your mouth. You can suck on me harder if you like it. Be rougher. Sloppier if you want. Everything you're doing feels good."

"Okay. Can you keep talking like that? Like you just did? That helps."

"Yeah, Madness. I can keep talking."

She gives me a half smile and then she returns to her rhythm, giving me more just like I asked.

"Fuck..." I groan. It's too good. Too perfect and I'm not going to last long like this. "Fuck me. Yes. You're so perfect, just like that. Use your tongue, right there. Oh fuck."

I have to bite back a loud moan. Terrified we're about to wake up someone in this house and have them running in here to find out what's wrong. Tobias will probably throw me to the mountain lion himself. But if this is out how I go out, it's worth it.

"You can squeeze a little tighter with your hand. Go a bit faster." She listens so carefully and carries out the orders so well. "Oh my god, Madness. Fuck. Yes—just like that."

I bite down hard on the inside of my cheek and concentrate on not rocking my hips forward. She's already getting me so close and I'm just trying to stay focused on not fucking this up for her. She's doing so well, it's hard to remember it's her first time. Except then I feel myself on the edge and I can't take much more. I didn't prepare for this part, so I grab a towel I'd left hanging over the edge of the bed.

"Fuck. Okay. I'm close. Let me take over."

She listens, releasing me and my breath stutters and I curse as I take over with my hand on the last few strokes. Coming hard while she watches me intently. My breathing is ragged in the wake of it and she quietly rises to her feet and then sits next to me on the edge of the mattress. I clean myself up and put my clothes back in order before I lay back on the bed. Trying to process how I just got some of the best head in my life from a complete novice.

She's looking me over carefully. Studying the mess she's made of me, no doubt wondering if it's been this easy to destroy a man all along.

"I could have swallowed." Her brow furrows in disappointment.

I laugh softly that that's the first thing she says.

"Not your first time. And probably not with me. It's already a lot to try to begin with, and that's not something everyone enjoys."

"Well, I don't know if I don't try. Right?" She smiles at me.

"True. But that's the sort of thing you try with a guy you like."

"I like you."

"Well, that's good considering everything we just did. Glad I pass the likability test."

She lays down next to me on the bed and looks over at me.

"I mean I like you enough to try. You're easy to like though. Easy to be around. And you're good to me. Thank you."

My heart skips full beats in my chest.

"Madness, you... I should be thanking you. Not the other way around."

"I just mean thank you for letting me try things with you. Like you said, most guys wouldn't want the awkwardness and you're really kind about everything. I just want you to know how much I appreciate it."

"Okay," I answer because I don't know what else to say.

The way she says it makes me feel like I've done something right. Something good even. It's been a long fucking time since I'd heard anything approaching praise out of anyone. I eat it up like I'm starved.

Anything that makes this girl feel good, I want to do more of. Anything that makes her think I'm good is the only thing I want to be doing with my life right now.

"Okay," she repeats and then leans forward and kisses my cheek. "I'll let you sleep. Don't forget to drink some more water though. You don't want a hangover."

"Yes boss," I grin at her as she climbs the ladder.

10

uentin

THE JEALOUSY SWIRLS in my gut as I watch her flirt with Xander while we play against each other out on the lawn. She tosses another bag to him and from here I can't hear their conversation. I can only see the way she laughs and the way his hand lingers a little too long on hers for my liking.

I shake my head. It's ridiculous. I'm ridiculous. She's not mine, and she was never going to be. She wanted Xander from the start. I was a steppingstone to help her get him, and acting like a jealous fool now is just going to make everyone wonder what the fuck is wrong with me. A thing they've been wondering enough lately.

"All right. You make this one, and we win." The girl from the grocery store whose name I've already forgotten is handing me a bag with one hand and rubbing her other over my forearm. She grins at me, and I can't tell if it's genuine interest on her part, or if she's seeing the same thing play out across the way that I am, and I'm her plan to make him jealous too.

I look at Xander as he lets out another laugh at whatever Madison's just said to him, another giggle following from her, and I think I might be fucking pissed at him. Want to slam my fist into his jaw for being such a fucking dreamboat that every woman we know seems to fall for him these days. I don't remember it being like this the last few years. We seemed to get our own fair share of interest. I never felt like it was a competition. But watching him with Madison? I feel like I might be sick.

"Right." I take the bag from Grocery Girl, and I chuck it hard. I swear I'm aiming for the board, but it lands square on the real target.

"Fuck!" Xander curses and looks up at me. His attention is torn away from Madison, and she looks up too.

"Oh shit!" I play stupid. "Guess that's one too many beers for me tonight." I force a laugh and Grocery Girl laughs with me, seemingly also happy that Xander and Madison's gigglefest has been interrupted.

"Yeah, aim's a little off buddy. Maybe a water next?"

"Or another beer." I chuck my empty one in the makeshift wastebasket we have out here. "Good game though. I'm heading inside."

He could win the game and win the girl. I glance over at Madison and then back at him. They'd be the perfect couple. Xander gives me a questioning look but doesn't move to stop me, and I'm more than happy to let him stay out here with his fan club. I can be happy for Madison without watching it unfold.

When I get inside, I have to duck around Tobias and his date making out and leaning against the kitchen counter to get my beer. I notice Shelby and her boyfriend are conspicuously absent too. I just hope they're not too loud tonight because I think it's just me, my bed, and my beer at this point while everyone else in this house fucks it out to their hearts' content. I can stare at the ceiling and imagine how great it'll be to see the first girl I can remember wanting this way at breakfast tomorrow morning after my best friend's had his way with her. It's perfect.

AT LEAST UNTIL twenty minutes later when I'm finished with my beer and the door swings open and then immediately closes. I see Madison's form as she tiptoes toward the beds like she's not sure if I'm awake or not. I don't even know what she's doing in here. Maybe hunting for lingerie or the condoms she picked up at the grocery store the other day. I don't move. I don't want to be asked for any last-minute tips or words of encouragement. It'll kill me.

"Quentin?" she whispers.

Fuck.

"Yep." I don't move, just close my eyes.

"You didn't come back out."

"I was tired."

"Oh." She sits down on the edge of the bed, and I can smell the perfume she put on earlier in the night. It mixes with her shampoo and that combination will haunt me for the rest of my life.

"Do you need something?" I crack my eyes open just enough to see her face. I'm silently begging her to have mercy on me.

She rolls her lower lip between her teeth and her eyes fall over me. I haven't changed for bed yet.

"I just thought... I don't know. Maybe you'd be up for something. But if you're tired..."

"Up for something?" I give her a look.

"Yeah. I mean... I thought maybe we could try another step."

I sit up slightly in bed, using my elbows to support me. I hate myself for what I'm about to say because I would love to invent another step if it meant I got more time with her. But I saw the way Xander's being with her tonight. If she ever has a chance, it's now. If I'm not going to be a completely selfish asshole, I won't steal that away from her.

"There aren't really any more steps to this. We've covered the basics."

"Oh... I just thought..." she trails off and looks back toward the door.

"And if you want him, you're losing your shot. Grocery Girl is jealous of you tonight."

"Jealous of me?"

"You and Xander were flirting pretty hard. You want him, go get him before she takes your spot."

"I wasn't flirting. We were just laughing about the game and something he was telling me about."

"Whatever the case... you should get out there."

"But I'm not ready."

Oh. Well fuck. I hadn't meant to pressure her.

"Oh okay. Well, that's fine. Wait until you are. You should still probably go out there and make some more jokes or something if you want to cock block her though." I offer Madison a smile. One I feel like I'm only half capable of.

"No, I mean... I think I'm ready for sex, just not with him." Her hand is on my thigh a second later, and I realize what she's asking. It's more than I can take tonight.

"I can't be your practice for Xander."

"Why not? We've done the rest."

"Because it's your first time. It should be with someone you really want." I have to be the bigger person here but fuck if it doesn't hurt to say.

"The rest was my first time too. I mean not the first few things but..." she trails off, and she studies my face.

"We probably shouldn't have done that either, but I got carried away."

"Is that what this is?" I see her eyes harden even in the dim light.

"I don't mean it like that, Madness. Fuck..." I reach for her hand, and she lets me take it. I swipe my thumb over the back of it. "I mean, you're so fucking smart and beautiful. I've never met anyone like you. I feel like an asshole for taking those things. I don't deserve them. Xander's a good guy. Selfless. Honest and thoughtful like you. You come from the same world. The two of you... it makes sense. It's why you like him. He wouldn't do anything to hurt you."

"But you would?"

"You make me want things I can't have."

"I just want you."

I barely have time to process her words before she ducks under the bed and climbs on top of me. Her legs straddle my thighs as her hands run under my shirt. She's everywhere all at once and my body lights like a fucking match under her touch.

I grab her hips and flip her over underneath me, pinning her down to the mattress, and I kiss my way up her throat and nip at her earlobe. She writhes underneath me, spreading her legs and canting her hips to meet mine. My cock is so fucking hard already. The thought of claiming her for myself. Making her mine. Hearing her cry out.

"You don't want me." I try to fight it.

"I do."

"What about Xander?"

"I don't care about Xander anymore. I want you, Quentin."

"You care about Xander. You were flirting with him tonight."

"Because you were flirting with *her*."

"I—what? You jealous, Madness?" I grin despite myself. For

some reason it amuses me. That this perfect fucking woman would be jealous over me—a fucking train wreck of bad decisions.

"Maybe."

"You like me," I say it out loud without thinking because the realization hits me like a ton of bricks.

"The way you are with me... No guy has ever treated me like you do. Like I matter. Like you care what I think and what I like. You make me laugh, and you make me come. You make me feel... everything, really. And I can't believe you hide it all like you do."

"Hide it all? I'm not hiding."

"You are. Pretending like you're not all the things Xander is. You're more." She whispers it in the darkness, and her hand goes to my heart, pressing her palm against my chest. It breaks something inside me that she thinks I'm such a good person. Especially when she's the last person who should think so.

"If I was more, I wouldn't have touched you in the first place. I fucking took advantage of you wanting help. Put my hands all over you." I brush her hair back and run my fingers down her throat and over her clavicle.

"Took advantage of me..." She laughs and rolls her eyes. "I might not have a lot of experience, but I'm not naïve. I wanted you to touch me."

"Then why everything about Xander?" I frown at her bemused expression.

"Easier to say that it was all about him than admit the truth. And when you were asking what I liked... you were also busy telling me all the things you like."

"Oh yeah?" I raise a brow.

"Yes. You like it when I run my nails over your skin. You like hearing me tell you how good you are. I'd joke that last part is about your ego, but I think you just haven't heard it enough to really believe it."

"Hearing it from you makes it feel real." I confess.

"Because it is. We are. I think."

Somehow her hand is through my chest, wrapped around my heart and I belong to her with just those few words. I'm gone. I'm hers.

11

Madison

His lips crash down on mine a moment later—the kind of kiss he's withheld from me before now. One that feels like he's worshipping me and devouring me in equal measure, and I want all of it. All of him.

His hands roam over my body, and I wrap a leg around his and my arms around his neck. I could care less about Xander or my brother or anyone that isn't Quentin. Because I've never felt the way I do with him. This sort of ache that melts through every inch of me. The way thoughts of him eat up every single moment of my day. How I crave every touch he'll give me. Whatever crush I had on Xander seems childish in comparison.

When he comes up for air, he buries his face against the crook of my neck with gentle intermittent kisses, and I can tell his mind is whirring with conflicted thoughts.

"I want you." I repeat the confession because I want him to know how true it is.

"You were drinking tonight," he argues.

"I had a beer. Nothing mind-altering." I huff in return.

"Fuck…" He groans and rolls off me, landing beside me on the narrow bed. "I want you Madison, but…"

I feel my heart sink.

"But what?"

"You waited this long for the right guy. What we did before is one thing, but this…"

"It doesn't matter that I think you're the right guy. I'm not allowed to decide that for myself?"

"You are." He takes a deep breath and closes his eyes. "This is what you want? Really?" He opens his eyes then and looks into mine. There's a seriousness there I can't miss. "To get it out of the way, so you can be free not to worry about it when you go on your trip?" I realize he's feeling vulnerable too. That this whole feelings thing might really be running both ways. My stomach tumbles with butterflies.

"No," I answer because now it's time to admit the truth. I don't want to do this without him knowing why. "That part's changed."

His dark blues catch mine and hold me with a piercing look.

"What's changed?"

"It's not about getting it out of the way anymore."

"No?" And I swear I see hope in his eyes. Which can't be possible.

"No. I want this. With you."

His eyes search mine. "I want you too."

I smile and lean over to kiss him softly. "So then have me."

"If you're sure. You have to be sure. I'll give you whatever you need to feel comfortable with this but anytime you're not, you say something. Okay?"

"I'm sure." I reassure him.

His lips are on mine again, kissing me in soft strokes as his hands wander down my sides. I reach absently for his shirt, pulling on the hem of it and he sits up. He tears it over his head, careful to avoid hitting the upper bunk and tosses it to the side while I do the same with my own. My fingers go to the clasps on my bra while he starts to work on his belt.

I'm distracted by how good he looks. How every muscle on his body moves and the way his tattooed skin looks in this light. The five o'clock shadow he has making every angle on his jaw look that much sharper. He catches me staring and his brow raises in question.

"You're really nice to look at." I grin at him as I slip my bra off. His eyes drift over my face and then down over my chest, falling to where my nipples start to bead up under his watch.

"Nothing compared to you. You're so gorgeous," he half-speaks, half-mutters the words as his hands run over my stomach. He leans over and kisses the underside of my breast and then makes his way over my rib cage and past my bellybutton to the top of my jeans.

He unbuttons them slowly, kissing his way along the top as he works and then gently tugging them down my hips as I lift off the mattress to help him. His lips return to me after he discards them. His fingers hook gently into the band of my panties to reveal more and more of me, his mouth kissing a trail in the wake of the retreating fabric. I close my eyes, trying to remember every moment of this. The way he makes me feel, the way he looks, the way he touches me—every single thing about this and how much I want him.

He kisses me softly and his tongue brushes over my clit in short gentle strokes until he has me wrapping my fingers around the edge of the pillow.

"You want more of this? We need you soaking wet before we

even think about trying. I don't want to hurt you." He glances up at me, looking positively devilish from this angle.

"Yes. I love the way you feel like this."

He wraps his fingers around the sides of my panties and slowly tugs them down my thighs and over my calves, tossing them to the side with my pants. It's not lost on me I'm totally naked now and he's still half dressed. It makes me feel a little self-conscious and he senses it, taking his pants and boxers off a moment later.

Seeing him like this, totally naked, and completely bared—it's a lot to take in. The tattoos that run over his arms and chest, down over his abdomen and flanking his sides are beautiful. His thighs look like they might be from one of the sculptures I was planning to spend time studying overseas. His dick is *a lot*. I don't have much to compare him too, but he's definitely bigger than the ones I've seen in person so far. He grins a little as he sees me surveying him. The brightness of his smile and the way his eyes glitter in this light—he's breathtaking. Every single part of him is and I can't help but think how lucky I am.

"Spread for me a bit more?" he asks as he slides back down between my thighs, just before his mouth lands on me again and I have to close my eyes and bite my tongue. The house is full of people and I don't want any of them coming in here to find us. That's my only regret—that we don't have the place to ourselves tonight.

His tongue teases over my clit and his fingers slip inside of me. I can feel how wet he's getting me and I concentrate on the way he feels. How all the little nerve endings in my body are lighting up under his touch. But my heart is starting to race and the nervous butterflies are there just under the surface when I think about what comes next.

"Talk me through it though? As we get close? It helps with my nerves," I whisper and he pauses in his ministrations to look up at me. His face studies mine and he kisses the inside of my thigh.

"We don't have to do anything you don't want to. If you're nervous about doing more I can make you come like this instead. Trust me, I love doing this every bit as much."

"No, I want to. I just like the way you talk me through things. It helps and it's... kind of sexy?" I let out a nervous laugh and he grins at me.

"I can try. Just if you're not sure, stop me?"

"I will. I promise."

He kisses me and then drags his tongue over me until I gasp, working me up again like he likes to see what sounds he can get out of me.

"You taste so good. I could have you like this every night and it would never be enough. I don't think you realize how perfect you are."

I feel a blush rise to my cheeks and I grin at him shyly but stay quiet until he starts to suck on my clit, my hips rising of their own volition desperately seeking more of him.

"Oh fuck..." I whisper, putting my hand over my mouth to stifle the small sounds I can't help.

His fingers work me gently along with his tongue and I can feel my orgasm starting to bloom when he pulls away from me.

"I want to make you come like this first. Please?"

The way he says please is almost enough to push me over the edge and make me say things I shouldn't. Confess that I've forgotten my brother even has another friend and that I might be in love with Quentin after all.

But instead I just nod my yes and his mouth returns to me. It doesn't take much. I'm chasing my release seconds later, pressing a pillow over my face and trying to blot out the noises I'm making. When he finally relents and the intensity of it starts to ebb, I pull the pillow away and a small laugh rumbles out of him as he kisses my stomach and studies me.

"You've got a messy hair thing going." He nods to me and I quickly brush my hair back with a sheepish grin.

"Oops." I shrug. "That was um... good?" I don't have words. He steals them away.

"Good, huh?" He smirks at me, pleased with the state he's put me in.

"Better than good."

"The sounds you make are better than good too."

I feel a little kick of pride that I'm not totally fucking this up so far, even though he was doing most of the work.

"What now?" I ask.

"Now..." He kisses my hip absently. "How do you feel?"

"Good."

"Too sensitive?" He brushes the pad of his thumb gently over my clit and I feel the little spark of it.

"A little sensitive but not too much."

"You want to try?"

"Yes."

"All right. I'm going to get a condom." He kisses me again and then disappears to his bag on the other side of the room. I hear the rip of foil and watch him move in the shadows before he comes back to the bed.

I lay back against the pillows again and spread my legs as he kneels between them, his eyes raking over my body.

"You're so gorgeous. And your body is honestly... I think it's all I'm going to see from now on." He leans over and kisses the inside of my knee before he comes down over me, his body inches from mine as I feel him between my legs.

"I've never wanted a guy the way I want you." I confess.

"I want you more than I can ever remember wanting anything in my life."

I bite my lip and smile up at him. Trying to stifle the giddiness I feel. "I'm glad it's you."

"Me too. I'll try to be gentle but you should know it won't

probably feel all that good for you the first time. It's going to hurt. If you want me to stop, just say so. I'll go slow, okay?"

"Okay." I nod.

He kisses down the side of my neck and his fingers slip between my legs and he brushes over my clit and slides them inside, testing me. I'm nervous but he makes me feel safe. He's been so careful with me this whole time that I trust him implicitly. So thankful that he's willing to be patient with me.

He lines himself up with me and I can feel the tip of him nudge against me. I take a breath and I spread my legs a little wider to accommodate him. He feels big. *Really* big. But then I'm a virgin, so I'm guessing anyone would feel big.

"Ready?"

"Ready."

He presses forward and I can feel him start to push inside. The tightness and a little twinge of pain. His hand drifts up and the pad of his thumb slips over my clit, gently swirling circles as he moves his hips. I close my eyes and try to focus on it. The way he draws up swells of desire at the same time as he stretches me.

"Breathe," he whispers. "This helps if you breathe. I don't want you to pass out on me."

I open my eyes and his brow is furrowed but there's a playful look in his blue eyes. I can't help the smile that follows.

"It's just *a lot*. You're *a lot*. Hurts a little."

"Do you want me to stop?" I can tell his tone is strained and he's working to go this slow with me.

"No. It's almost in, right?" I ask.

There's a soft deep sound of his chest like he's trying to stifle a laugh.

"Madness, I'm barely inside at all. You're just tight as fuck. We can stop if it doesn't feel good. I don't want you to hurt."

"It's okay. I knew it would hurt. I did research. Remember?"

"Yeah. You did research." He grins. "Focus on where it feels good. Does this help?" The pad of his thumb circles over my clit again.

"Yes," I let out a little gasp when he hits a sensitive part, and I rock my hips forward, taking more of him in the process.

"Oh fuck..." He groans and his eyes shutter. "I... You... You feel so fucking good."

"Just do it." I implore him because I don't want him to keep having to hold back for me. "I want you. Please. Just fuck me, Quentin."

"Fuck, okay..." he whispers back before his full concentration returns to where he's just inside of me.

He eases himself in and I can tell from the way he's breathing that he's going as slowly and carefully as he can manage. I close my eyes because I feel so full of him that I might burst. But I keep concentrating on where he's working me up to another orgasm. Focusing on the fact that I have Quentin Undergrove between my thighs. That my first time doing this is with *him*.

"There. Fuck..." he curses again and then he looks down at me just as I open my eyes. "How do you feel?"

"I don't know. How do I feel?" I tease him, hoping to break the tension that's got his brow all wrinkled.

He grins in response. "Like I don't deserve you."

"Well I'm yours either way."

"Lucky me." His eyes search mine for a moment. "I'm going to move. If it—"

I slip my hand over his mouth. "I know. I'll tell you. From now on just say dirty things, okay? I'll tell you if I need something."

He kisses my palm and starts to move. It's an exquisite sort of pain when he does. Half-pleasure, half-soreness. I run my hands over his shoulders, feeling the muscles work as he fucks me and listening to the soft moans of his gratification. Loving that I'm the reason for it.

"Fuck. You're so tight, Madness. You feel perfect."

"You feel massive."

A laugh rumbles out of him. "Just what every guy wants to hear."

"Just don't break me." I laugh, my fingers playing over his shoulders. His face turns serious then, like maybe I've said the wrong thing. His eyes study mine and then hold me when he speaks again.

"I won't break you. Don't break me?"

My heart pounds in my chest at the idea this man thinks I have any ability to make him feel anything that strongly and I nod. "Deal."

He kisses me and I wrap one of my legs around him as he starts to fuck me with a little more force, picking up his pace like he's finally relaxing. His lips leave my mouth and make their way over my jaw and down my throat.

"I'm not going to last much longer. You feel too good. So fucking tight and wet."

"It's okay. It feels better. Less pain, more.... Good?" I muse at my lack of vocabulary right now. Jane would have had way better words while she was losing her virginity. "But I don't think I can come again. Just worry about you. I want to feel you come."

"You sure? I can use my mouth again? We can try something different?"

"I just want to feel you." I shake my head because it's true. I don't care about me right now. What I want is seeing Quentin come apart while he's inside me. Knowing it was because of me. For me.

"Okay," he agrees reluctantly.

It doesn't take much longer and I can feel his body shudder. A low moan rolls out of him and there's deep intake of breath. He pulls out of me another moment later and I feel a little pang at the loss of him.

"You okay?" His eyes open and he studies me. Something there on his face I can't quite read. His fingers play with my hair and I kiss his palm.

"I'm good. Are you good?"

He kisses me softly without answering, so tender it almost feels like he wants to be sure I know how much he cares about me. That this is more than just sex for him. I kiss him back for a few moments and then he lets me go, catching my breath and letting my mind come down from the high of all this. He rolls to the side and then sits up.

"Let me take care of the condom."

He gets up again, disappearing into the shadows on the far side of the room while I slip my panties and a tee back on. I don't know what women he fucks normally do at this point. Probably slink back to their dorm rooms or head back out to whatever party they're at. I think I need a minute to myself before I do or say anything stupid so I grab my jeans and start putting them on.

When he comes back he looks at me with a question before he starts to dress too.

"I'm just going to run to the bathroom." I explain.

"Okay." He nods but he watches me out of the corner of his eye.

WHEN I GET BACK to the bedroom a few minutes later, he's lying on the bed waiting for me. His eyes jump to mine as soon as I walk in the room and start to get undressed for bed.

"I don't know how this part goes." I shrug, giving him a nervous smile.

"It goes however you need it to go. You want to come sit here with me for a minute?"

I walk over and slide into the bunk bed next to him, staring at the slats under the bed above us.

"You don't have to give me a pep talk or anything. I'm good. A little sore but good."

"Are you sure? If you want to talk, we can."

"I don't need to talk. I can let you sleep."

"Madness, if you don't talk I'm going to get nervous. You always talk. What we did was a big thing for you. A big thing for me too, really. I want to be sure you're okay."

"I just... kind of don't want to ruin it by talking? I don't think I have great words right now and I... It was special and you were perfect. Everything I wanted." I look over at him and he's watching me again, studying me like he wants to be sure I'm telling him the truth.

"Okay," he whispers, tucking a strand of my hair behind my ear and running his thumb over my jaw. "We don't have to talk. But stay in this bed with me?"

"I can do that." I smile at him and he turns to his side and wraps his arm around my middle. My heart tumbles and I have to fight from kicking my feet because this might be new for me, but I know that this means something. That I mean something to him.

"Good." He kisses my forehead and I fall asleep in his arms, the happiest I can remember being in a long time.

12

Quentin

THE NEXT MORNING I'm half-awake when I feel her stir in my arms. Her ass is nestled against me, and her skin is warm and soft against mine. We're both still curled up under the covers, squashed together in this tiny bed, the sun just starting to pour in through the window and everything about this—everything about her—feels right. Feels perfect if I'm being honest with myself.

She grins at me over her shoulder and turns to face me, kissing me softly and pressing her curves against my body as she moves one leg over mine and tucks it back under my calf. I kiss her back for several minutes until it turns into more than just kisses, her hands searching over my skin and her hips rocking forward until she grazes over my cock. I'm already going hard, and she's wetter than she should be for that little bit of foreplay.

"Aren't you sore?" I whisper as I kiss my way down her neck.

"A little."

"We should take it easy then."

"So just my mouth on you then?" She gives me a devious grin and starts to slide down my body, pulling the sheets with her, and the cool air from the air conditioning whips over my skin, contrasting with the warmth of her between my thighs as her hands wrap around me. She slides her tongue over the tip of my cock, teasing me with just a taste of her mouth a moment later.

"Fuck, your mouth is so good..." I groan, my eyes starting to slide closed.

A hard rap of knuckles against the door startles me, and a moment later the door opens. Madison and Tobias's father, Coach Westfield, fills the frame with his imposing presence.

"Okay. Just get dressed, Tobias." His head turns in slow motion, and he starts speaking before his eyes can focus on us. "Madison, get up honey. I got here early. We're gonna go get some breakfast—" He stops mid-sentence. His eyes going wide and then his nostrils flare.

Madison squeals and pulls the covers over her head, diving down next to me but still leaving them woefully short of covering my face. So I'm stuck staring at Coach Westfield while he's getting so red, I think he might actually be about to have a heart attack.

"Undergrove, if that's my fucking daughter under that sheet and not some whore you picked up from a bar, I will kill you myself."

Madison's arms wrap around me, and she pops up from under the sheet. Fury on her face, and her blonde hair a wild mess from the sex we had last night and being under the covers just now.

"You aren't killing anyone. And you can mind your own business."

"You are my fucking business." He pinches his nose. "Jesus fucking Christ. Can you children not act like you have some sense for a few fucking days in a row. One of you will fucking kill me."

"What the fuck is going on?" Tobias has appeared next to his father and peers over his shoulder. His eyes dodge between me and Madison, cycling through the various forms of outrage —shock, disbelief, and finally anger of his own. His jaw tightens, and his eyes land firmly on me.

"Our father thinks he can tell me what to do with my vagina."

"Your vagina. Jesus Christ Madison." Coach Westfield slams his hand against the frame of the door. "Get fucking dressed. And you." He points to me. "You get your fucking ass out of my goddamn house. I told Tobias you were trash a long time ago." He turns to Tobias and shoves past him. "Maybe now you'll fucking believe me instead of acting like you know every goddamn thing under the sun."

Tobias opens his mouth to protest and then thinks better of it, closing it again and returning his attention to us.

"You can't let Dad talk to him like that. He is *not* trash. And what I do with my body isn't Dad's fucking business." Madison is a ball of rage next to me.

"Get dressed Mads." Is all Tobias says, his eyes shifting to mine. The slightest shake of his head when he looks at me is all I need to see to know that our friendship is over.

Tobias closes the door behind him, and Madison turns to me. Her eyes are frantic as she looks at me, tears welling in them.

"I'm so sorry. Don't listen to him. He's an asshole. And Tobias will get over it. I'll explain everything."

"What will you explain?" I ask softly, slowly coming to grips with the fact that I've well and truly fucked things up now.

"That you... that I like you, and this was all my idea."

"Your idea was for me to help you seduce Xander. I don't think we should tell them that." I get out of bed and grab my pants, slipping them on and my shirt while she continues.

"That was just an excuse. I told you. I liked you—like you. I... I have feelings for you, Quentin, and I don't regret anything. My dad has a temper, and I know our families don't get along, but he'll get over it. I promise. He takes time but eventually, he listens to me. I'm good at talking him down. Better than my brothers honestly. Better than even my mom. Just give me a chance to talk to him."

I'm already putting my stuff in my bag, and I can hear the panic start to seep into her voice. But I know it doesn't matter. Even if she could talk her dad down. He hates me. And he'll hate that I slept with his daughter. Then there's Tobias. He'll never believe that I did it because I have feelings for her. That I like her. He'll think I just took what was in front of me like I usually do. Because I have no self-control and my self-loathing runs deep. It might hit a new level today though, facing the cold light of morning where I've fucked over one of my best friends by hiding all of this from him instead of telling the truth. His father will use it against him for a long time to come.

"Madison, it's okay."

"Don't call me Madison. That's not what you call me." She stands, and I glance back at her and have to rip my eyes away. This is probably the last time I see her, and I don't want to remember her crying like this, miserable because of me. I want to be able to close my eyes and see her like she was this morning—happy and sweet as she kissed me back.

"Nothing you say is going to calm your dad and brother down right now. Right now, I need to get out of here."

We both look to the door when we hear the sound of raised voices again and then footsteps down the hall. The door opens a moment later and Madison jumps back, pressing the T-shirt I dropped last night to her chest as a cover. It's Xander in the doorway. His eyes flick to her, and when he sees the tears, they turn on me, hard-set like I'm the biggest piece of shit he's ever seen.

"If you're not out of this fucking house in five minutes, I'll give you the beating they won't."

Madison gasps, but I just nod and keep chucking my stuff in my bag. Xander slams the door behind him, and I hear his footsteps retreat. Madison grabs clothes out of her own bag and changes into them quickly before she comes back to me. She puts her hands over my bag to stop me from putting anything else in it.

"Quentin please," she begs. "Just give them a minute to cool down and let me talk to them. Stay in here, and I'll handle it. I'll make them see it's fine. That I'm fine."

"Xander meant what he said, and I don't really want broken bones on top of my other problems right now Madi—Madness. Just let me get out of here. That'll help them cool down."

"Where are you going to go? You don't have a car."

"I can walk to town and get a ride from there. I got a ride on the way here. I can do it on the way out."

"Please don't leave. If you have to go for a minute, okay. But please don't leave town. I want to talk with you. We didn't talk last night. We said we'd talk today. Please don't leave without that." She's pulling out all the stops because the fact that I want to run as fast as I can from all of this probably shows on my face.

I can't take it. I want to cry myself, and it's the last thing I need to do in front of her. She's trusted me this entire time to be the experienced one. The guy who knows what he's doing. The guy who won't let her down. The one who's good for her. And I don't want to fail her now by losing my shit.

"Quentin." Her fingers slip under my jaw, and she stands. I straighten with her, biting the insides of my cheek as I look at her, willing myself not to cry.

"Yeah, Madness?" I force a smile.

"Don't leave without talking with me, okay? You promised me that you'd give me whatever I needed. I need this."

I nod. "Okay."

I don't know how I'll keep that promise. *If* I can keep the promise. I'm fairly certain her father is going to throw her into the back of an unmarked car and ship her off to a convent after this. Might be a nice one in Europe, but I'm sure he'll keep her far away from me. And Tobias will be the one to drive it.

She leans forward and kisses my cheek. "Thank you. I'll fix this. I promise. It's my fault, and I'll fix it."

"It's not your fault. I should have been more careful with you. With this... I'm sorry I caused this." I lean back down and zip the bag. "Don't fight with your family over me. Okay? They're just trying to protect you. Especially Tobias."

"Quentin..." Her fingers slip over my forearm as I head out the door.

I force another smile. "I'm fine. Truly. Don't worry about me. Just take care of you."

"And you'll wait to talk with me?"

"I'll wait." I nod, and then I take off down the hall. I don't look up the whole way out. I'm too ashamed of myself. Of how greedily I acted. Of how much I tried to take what I didn't deserve. I can feel Tobias's and Xander's eyes on me as I leave, and I feel my gut churn. This was supposed to be all of us having one last weekend together now that they're going off to the pros and now it's just one more reason for them to be disappointed in me.

I knew saying goodbye would be hard—but going out like this makes it feel like goodbye forever.

13

Madison

I'VE NEVER BEEN MORE embarrassed in my life than I am right now. Between having my father walk in on me half naked in Quentin's bed and having him act like Quentin is the scum of the earth, screaming at me even more after he leaves, I just want to crawl under the covers and never come back out again. But first I want to find Quentin. I want to apologize for the absolute shitshow of a family circus he had to endure, and I want him to know it doesn't change anything for me. Even if it might for him.

I call his phone for the tenth time, and it goes straight to voicemail. He can't have gone far. There's no easy way out of here and he'd need to find a ride before he could. So he has to have walked somewhere in town to find it, and I'm determined to go to every business I can until I find him.

It doesn't take long. My guess is that he might have ended

up at a bar to drown out the memories of this morning and bury any good thoughts he might have had about me. I'm sure he regrets agreeing to help me. Regrets last night. He probably even regrets coming up to the house to see his friends all over again. My cheeks go red at the thought of my dad yelling at him next to me in bed. I'm sure being walked in on by a girl's father is a brand-new experience he hasn't had before. At least I could give him one of his firsts.

I spot him alone at the bar, drinking a beer and staring up at the TV. I say a little prayer to the gods of awkwardness that I get through this without too much of it. Because holy hell have I had enough of it today, and then I make my way across the bar, gently touching his forearm when I get to him.

"Hey," I say softly, starting this all out really strong.

His eyes light with the recognition, and he looks behind me immediately, like he's worried I'll have the same entourage of men behind me I did earlier today.

"It's just me," I reassure him and his face relaxes a bit with the information.

"You shouldn't be here."

"I needed to talk with you."

"How'd you get here?"

"Walked."

"You walked? Your brother and dad are going to be losing their fucking minds. We should get you home." He starts to stand.

"It's fine. I told them I was going on a long walk, and I didn't want to speak with any of them." I shake my head, my cheeks going pink. "After this morning, I don't know if I ever want to see any of them again." Instinctively I press my hand to the back of Quentin's, and he stares down at it.

"It's my fault. Don't be mad at them."

"How is it your fault?"

"I shouldn't have touched you in the first place."

I recoil and take a step back. "Now you're on their side?"

He looks at me, and his face softens when he sees mine. "No, I don't mean it like that. I mean... Fuck. I mean I don't deserve you, Madison. You're so fucking perfect. So smart and sweet. So kind. Just so many fucking things I'm not. They're just trying to protect you from me."

"I don't want to be protected from you. I'm in love with you." The second I blurt out the words he freezes and it feels like time stops. His eyes search mine, and I'm silently pleading with him to forget I said anything even though that's impossible now.

But he grabs me a moment later and his lips slam down on mine, his arms wrapping around me and pressing me close. I melt into him, and I can hear a whistle from the other side of the mostly empty bar. I'm sure it's one of the locals enjoying the midday show. He pulls away a moment later though and stares down at me—something so vulnerable on his face that it makes the blue in his eyes bright enough that I can hardly look back at him.

"Do you mean it?" he asks.

"Yes."

"You're sure?"

"I'm sure but—"

"I love you too. This is all moving so fast, but I just... you're nothing like I've ever known, Madness. You make me feel like I can't think straight. Can't think about anything but you." He kisses me again, softer this time.

"They don't matter to me. Their opinions don't matter to me. I just want you." I wrap my arms around his neck and press my head to his chest. He squeezes me tight.

"I wish I could say the same. But I want what's best for you every bit as much as I want you. I don't know if that's me. I want it to be, but I don't know." His voice shakes a little bit as he talks and I can tell this is as new for him as it is for me.

That he's going to need my reassurance as much as I need his.

"It's you. I've never felt like this either. That can't be a coincidence can it. That we both feel so strongly about it like this? That everything between us has been so easy. I just know I love you."

"Madness..." There are tears forming in his eyes and he squints like he's in pain before he hugs me again. "I love you. But I don't know how we fix this."

"Well right now, I think we get out of this bar. Pay off your tab and find some place for us to stay. We can't go back right now obviously. But we can figure it out. We'll figure something out. I'm not letting them separate us."

"Is that what they want?"

"Dad wants me to go home. I told him no way was I leaving. That it's my summer vacation and he's being ridiculous."

"I don't want to piss him or Tobias off any more than I already have."

"He just needs time to process. Tobias I mean. He'll understand. Dad might not ever get it, but he'll come around to accept it eventually. He always does. He'll see what a good person you are just like I have."

"I doubt that."

"I don't. Now let's go."

We finish paying off his tab and wander our way to the edge of town. There's a small unassuming place that has cabins for rent along the river and I use my card to check us in when I see him falter over his own wallet. He doesn't protest but I can tell he feels like shit about it, and I reassure him several times that it's fine. It's just one of the many things we're going to figure out. Once we're in the cabin I get him water and something to eat from the vending machines, letting him have some lunch while I explain what happened after he left.

"I wish I'd handled this differently." He says at last, the food hitting his system hard and the sobered look on his face hurts my heart.

"I wish we'd just told Tobias. Other than that, I don't care. What I do and who I do it with isn't anyone's business. I'm grown. I only wish we'd told Tobias because he's your friend."

"I wish we'd said something too. I need you to know Madness… I don't regret you or what we did. Not for a second, but I regret that I fucked up so badly in how we handled it. How I handled it really…"

"I wanted you to keep it a secret. You were keeping my confidence like I asked you to. I liked it that way. And it was fun… and sexy. And… I don't know. I don't know how honest Lana and Lo were being but you made everything amazing for me. I don't think many women can say that."

"Well, I'm glad I'm good for something." He grins.

14

uentin

"You're good for everything, Quentin. I want to be with you. I love you and I... I just want to be with you."

"I want to be with you too. But I don't know how that's possible. Even without your dad and Tobias furious. I have to figure out my life and you're set to leave for your trip."

"Right. The trip... What if you just came to Europe with me?" She looks up at me bright-eyed. Like it's the best idea she's had in a while. Like we might get the happily ever after she's always believed in.

I hate that I have to crush her spirit.

"I wish I could but... I can't afford that. I really have to figure out what I'm doing. Where my career is going. It's do or die for me right now. Either trying to go back and figure out a way to pay for the next year so I can hopefully get off the bench or going back to work for me."

"Right. I'm sorry. That was a stupid question."

"It wasn't stupid. I'm... Honestly it feels amazing that you would even ask me to go with you. I'd love to but I've got to get my life in order. I've made a mess of it... If we were ever going to have a shot, Madness. I'd have to unfuck so many things right now that I'm not sure how to fix."

"Well... I'm here. We can fix them together. I can help you fix them. I'm good at that sort of thing. Easton and Tobias have needed me more than once to help them smooth things over with our parents or some girl they were seeing. Once when Easton had a problem with a teacher and was going to fail out of a class too. I helped talk her out of it."

"Yeah... I can see that about you. I bet you get everyone around to your side of things. Get them to see it how you do. You're very convincing." I was fairly certain this girl could talk me into jumping off a cliff.

"Usually. So let me help you. We can fix it. You're so talented and smart. You're a good guy, Quentin. Everyone knows it. You just made a few mistakes. We all do that. It's just a matter of figuring out how to fix them and then make up for them. It's not the end of the world. I'm sure we can figure it out."

I honestly believe her in this moment. That my whole life falling apart isn't nearly as bad as I've made it out to be. That between the two of us we can get out of it. I'm desperate to hear her ideas, because I just want some way that this story ends with me getting a chance at this girl. With me having a career that might give us an actual shot together.

"Okay. We can try."

She breaks out a notebook and pen from her purse a moment later and starts working with me to brainstorm ideas. Nothing, she claims, is too small or too stupid of an idea. We just have to figure out which one is best and to do that we have to put down anything we can think of.

We spend the whole afternoon and into the evening

working on her list until I finally beg her to take a break and come get dinner with me. We walk to one of the local diners and get something to go, setting up a picnic on the table that's behind the cabin. It overlooks the river and with her curled up on the bench, the sounds of the water and the smell of the pines in the evening, even though everything has gone to shit, it feels like in this moment, everything's right.

She's staring thoughtfully out over the water when I nudge her gently.

"Penny for your thoughts."

"I have an idea. I think it would fix everything. But I don't think you're going to like it."

"What's that?"

She looks back at me, her eyes searching mine for a moment before she says the last thing I'm expecting.

"Marry me."

I choke on the sip of my drink I've just taken. Sputtering and coughing and having to grab a napkin to dab it away. When I'm finished she's still looking at me like she's serious.

"I'm sorry, *what*?" I look at her like she's lost her mind.

"It would fix a bunch of our problems. Yours. Mine. Give us a chance to be together."

"Madness. People are usually together awhile before they decide to get married. Like it works the other way around, you know?"

"Sure. But sometimes desperate times call for desperate measures."

"I don't think I like being described as desperate."

"I didn't mean that you're desperate. Just that the situation is. Anyway, do you want to hear the idea or not?" She raises a brow at me like I'm a misbehaving toddler.

"I want to hear it."

"We get married. It stops all this chatter from my dad, Tobias, and Xander. They see we're serious. That you didn't take advantage of me and that I want to be with you because I love you. Then, I sell the tickets and stuff I have for the Europe trip. That'll give us enough money to make a start. We can pay for whatever tuition you need to pay for with that money. I looked up the tuition cost and even if you have no scholarship after this—it'll work. My plane ticket when it's cashed out will cover almost all of it. It would be a big gift if I just gave it to you, but if we're married—it's just joint money. And when you're drafted in the pros next year, it'll be pennies in comparison."

She takes a breath, searching my face before she continues.

"We'll move back to your university town and you'll play football. I'll either get a job or start attending classes. Maybe both. But if we're married we could live in the family student housing. It'd be a lot cheaper and mean we don't have to pay for separate dorms or an apartment. I might even be able to get a discount on tuition with you being an athlete. And between football and me, you'll be too busy to get into any sort of trouble. I can help you with homework and managing your schedule so you don't have to feel like you're pulled in so many directions. You can focus on getting off the bench and back into your coach's good graces. Plus it'll give me a chance to explore what I want to do with my future without worrying about what my dad thinks or wants for me. The pressure of living up to my family legacy and my brothers. I'd be Madison Undergrove not Madison Westfield... It's perfect, really."

She finishes her speech and then looks to me for my reaction, and I'm mildly stunned. She's thought it through. Researched it. Run numbers. I'd taken a break or two from her brainstorming session and apparently she'd used that time to formulate a plan. A complete one where our lives are on track. I wasn't sure the living bit would work since I normally lived in athlete housing. But it might.

"I mean... After you're drafted, you could divorce me if you wanted. I wouldn't contest it. We could sign paperwork or whatever. Then we could start over... try the couple thing like normal. Just date."

"Madness... I'm not going to have you make all those sacrifices for me and then divorce you."

"So you agree that it's a good idea?"

"I don't know if it's a good idea, but you definitely thought it through."

"Why isn't it a good idea?"

"Because it's... practical to a fault. It's not passion or love driving you to want to marry me. It's trying to get us out of this situation and I don't know that that's a great start to a marriage or even a relationship. It's not that I hate the idea of being married to you. I don't. I like the idea, honestly."

"Well good," she interrupts. "I'm glad I pass the likability test."

I laugh a little then and it breaks some of the tension.

"I'm just saying I think that marriage is the kind of thing you go into because you can't imagine being without that person. Not the kind of thing you do because it's a way to solve a problem in the moment. Besides, I think some of that stuff we could get around without being married."

"We could. But it would be harder. Also... Right now, I can't imagine being without you. Leaving you here or you going back to wherever it is you're going to hitch a ride to."

"Well I hate the idea of you going off on a gap year. Especially if there are other more talented guys involved," I try to tease her but she gives me a look that tells me she's not amused.

"Like I said Madness..."

"We've solved every other problem so far together by being practical. Your advice was practical. Your teaching me was practical. So far practical's turned out really well for us. Or at least really well for me..." She grins.

"I mean, me too..." I can't argue with that.

"So... Marry me." She repeats.

I shake my head and stare back out over the river. Contemplating the idea she's proposed. All the sacrifices she'd be making. But if it worked out, if I could hold it together this last year and get back on track to being drafted, I'd be able to pay her back tenfold. A year from now we could be moving into a house in a new city. She could be going to any school she wants. We could spend next summer traveling and letting her explore to decide what she wants to do. I could give her anything she wants and get her out of the shadow of her father and her family name.

I should think she's crazy for even mentioning the idea, let alone asking. I should feel awkward that this girl who's younger than me is proposing to save my life right now—and quite literally proposing to marry me. But it feels right. She feels right in a way I can't imagine happening twice in one lifetime. The alternative of giving her up sounds bleak and I can't imagine walking away from her. Not when the alternative is that I get to be with her for as long as she'll have me. So it might just be time to fall in with fate.

"Okay."

"Okay?" She gives me a hopeful look, one that's surprised but excited.

"You have some good points. We can talk about it."

"We can go apply for the license in town today. This is a county seat. Then we can just sign the paperwork and it's done."

"What?" I blink at her. "Don't we need like a preacher or a judge or something?"

"No. We can marry ourselves. We just need some witnesses but I bet we can find some. Back at the bar if nowhere else."

"That easy?"

"That easy." She nods.

I might have had more reservations if I'd known how

quickly this would fall into place. But now that I've agreed, I'm not about to back out on her.

Which is exactly how I find myself with a marriage license and a couple of strangers in a park. Just before I hear her father yell her name in the distance.

15

uentin

Coach Westfield's bright blue eyes blaze as he looks down his nose at me.

"I'm just going to be straight with you, son."

"I'm not your son."

"I'm well aware, and it's going to stay that way. Whatever it takes."

I clench my fist, running my thumb over my knuckles under the table. I'm fairly certain punching a pro ball coach will get you kicked off any future draft lists.

"Just say what you want to say."

He looks me over again, his eyes scanning my skin where my tattoos are and shakes his head. Doesn't matter that his own son has nearly as many, I'm still trash and worse yet, trash with the wrong last name. He glances out the window and then back at me.

"Your uncle should have raised you better. Man's a fucking asshole, but he could have done better by you after what happened to your father."

I don't say anything. I love my uncle. He kept me off the streets, gave me a place to stay, and helped me get into college with a scholarship. I couldn't ask for more than that. I wasn't one of his kids. And he and my dad didn't exactly get along.

"At least he recognized your talent. Even if you're determined to piss it away with all your extracurricular bullshit."

I clench my jaw and shift in my seat. "Is there a point to this? If you want to talk me into staying away from your daughter, it won't happen. I love her."

"Love her?" He laughs. "You don't know the first thing about love if you think whisking a nineteen-year-old girl, with her whole future ahead of her, off to get married is love. You don't even know her."

"I know everything about her I need to know. I *love* her. I didn't whisk her away. It was her idea."

"Because she's fucking nineteen years old, and you're the first man to give her attention. She doesn't love you. She's in love with the idea of you. When she wakes up to the reality—and trust me she will—she won't want it. I'd guess if you treat your grades the same way you treat staying on the field, you're probably barely floating by. One more infraction you'll be off the team and you don't have the grades or the money to stay in school. So you'll be on the street—a high school grad like a million other guys out there trying to find some shitty nine-to-five that barely pays the bills. Maybe, if you're lucky, you could be like your old man—get a mechanic job that at least lets you drive an old beat-up piece of shit around town. Living in some roach-infested apartment, no savings, no prospects, barely able to feed the two of you. You think she loves you enough to live like that?"

I don't answer. My throat's tightening and the nausea starts to fill my belly.

"Or do you think she starts to regret the fact she didn't go to college? Starts to miss having a credit card with no limit. Catches the attention of other men while she's working at whatever dive bar she's forced to wait tables at to help pay the rent. Probably one with a lot more sense and money than you. As pretty as she is. Might take a month, tops."

"You've got her wrong if you think she's like that."

"Oh, I know my girl. She's as loyal as they come. Like a fucking rottweiler for the people she cares about. She defends her brothers enough, trust me. She'll stay with you. Even as things get bleaker and bleaker. While she watches her whole life pass her by and all she has to show for it is a shitty job and no future. Her friends will move on. Her brothers will go on to play in the pros. She'll come home for the holidays and see everything she left behind. Catch up with old friends to hear all about the adventures they're having and the jobs that afford them basic things like cars and houses. Her brothers will offer her help. They both have the kind of hearts that won't want to see her suffer and she won't take it. She wouldn't want to embarrass you like that, damage your ego even more than it already will be watching your friends play in the pros while you sit around on Sunday talking about what could have been. She'll tell you you're perfect the way you are. Do anything to keep your ego inflated. So she'll make herself small. Force herself to fit into your tiny fucking world. And you'll have to watch it all happen. Know that it was you who took all the opportunities for a bright future away from her. Someone who could give her a life that she truly deserves. That what you want?"

I turn to look out the window. The acid in my stomach rises up my throat.

"I didn't think so. And I think you know, somewhere—deep down, that I'm right. So I'm going to give you another option.

One that gives you both a better future. You pack your shit and you leave. Leave her a short note. I'll give it to her. Tell her you changed your mind. That she's too young for you, and you're not ready to settle down after all. Then you never contact her again. In exchange, I'll help you get transferred to a different college. Get you a clean slate where you can use your last year and that last name of yours to prove you're draft-worthy. Give you a chance to get into the pros and not end up in the gutter. Give her a chance to have all the opportunities she deserves. Ones she's worked her whole young life for. Let her chalk this up to lessons learned about men like you. You both get a future you deserve."

I'm not sure if it's possible to feel your own heart shatter, but if it is—I am. My chest is so tight, I almost can't breathe, and my heart feels like it's in a vice. Skipping to a beat I don't recognize. Because while every bone in my body wants to rebel, I just keep picturing her in that shitty apartment bogged down with all the worries she's never had to deal with in her life. Ones I lived with through my whole childhood until my dad got locked up and my uncle took me in. The same things that drove my mom to California and left me on my uncle's porch with a duffel bag. Things I wouldn't wish on anyone. Least of all Madison.

"You know I'm right." Coach Westfield drives in the coffin nails one by one with the stamp of the back of his pen on the table. "She deserves more. I think whatever your intentions were with her, you know that much."

I stare at the floor for a long while, trying to imagine a world where Madison ends up better off with me. But I can't see it. Instead, I just see the light slowly dimming in her eyes with the creep of time. When I continue to disappoint her, and she continues to lose one opportunity after another that she could have had without me.

"Do you have a piece of paper?" I ask at last.

16

Madison

"Get your bags packed. Let's go." My father opens the door and motions for me to hurry up.

"Go where?" I glare at him.

"Back to the airport. We're going home. Going to get this trip rescheduled for you and get you back on the road."

"Uh, no we're not. I'm staying here until I see Quentin. Where is he?"

"He left."

"What do you mean he left?"

"Exactly what I said. He's gone. Now let's go. I don't have time for any more shenanigans out of you, Madison. And don't think about calling your mother for sympathy. She's as furious as I am."

My heart crashes to a halt in my chest. Quentin couldn't have left. Wouldn't have left. There's no way. I know when he said he loved me he meant it. I could see it in his eyes. Feel it in the way he talked to me.

"No. He wouldn't."

"Well, he did. Now pack your bags."

I push past my father into the main room of the house, and I see my brother on the couch. His eyes are on his phone.

"Tobias, where's Quentin?"

Tobias looks like he's been over the coals too. I can't imagine Dad didn't blame him in part for all of this. He never wanted Tobias talking to someone with the last name Undergrove in the first place, let alone being friends with him and bringing him into his house. God forbid he touch his daughter.

"I don't know, Mads." Tobias shakes his head and looks back down at his phone.

I whip around to see my father standing there now, still looking as pissed off and as formidable as ever. I hate him in this moment. I'd never thought he was the best father. He was frequently absent, always focused on football over his family, and his betrayal of my mother—even if it resulted in one of my favorite people in the world—was something that always hung over this family like a pall. But occasionally he had moments. Times when he felt like he was a real dad. Teaching me how to throw a football. Making time occasionally when I was in high school to show up to my volleyball games and cheer me on—even if his presence was as much a distraction as it was a reward. When he picked me up from my first car accident in my new car and told me it was just a car that could be fixed rather than yelling at me. Those moments had always given me enough to cling to. But now I can't help the sneaking suspicion he's done something to Quentin. Forced his hand.

"What did you say to him?" I stare at Dad, feeling the burn of tears at the back of my throat.

"I told him he wouldn't get any money out of marrying you. That was all I needed to say."

It breaks me.

"I hate you. You ruin *everything*. Just because you don't know how to love someone doesn't mean you have to ruin it for everyone else."

"I ruin everything? Everything you have is because of me, and you take it all for granted. I've been too soft on you. Your mom wanted you to stay in college. I was the one who thought you trying your gap year might get your head on straight. But instead when we give you an inch, you take a mile. Shacking up with some piece of shit felon's boy who only wanted your money. I thought you were brighter than falling for that. Instead, you embarrass yourself, me, and your brother. I'm done letting you run wild. Pack your shit."

"Don't bring me into it," Tobias warns, standing from his place on the couch.

"I'm not going with you."

"Madison." I see my father's face turning its signature red. The one the sportscasters always comment on when he's lost his patience with the refs. I can see him gearing up to unleash hell.

"I'll take her home," Tobias interrupts.

My dad silently turns and looks at Tobias. There's an exchange between them, a silent one.

"Today," my father says before he gives me one last withering glare and storms out of the room.

I look at Tobias and then I feel the tears come crashing through. I can't hold them back anymore. The pride that I still had in front of my dad is gone now that it's just me and Tobias. He crosses the room and wraps his arms around me.

"It's gonna be okay, Mads."

"It's not. Nothing is okay. I love him. Really love him. I'm not stupid. He loves me too. Dad, he ruins everything. You know he ruins everything good."

"Well, we'll see. Just... for now, let's get you packed and out of here, okay?" Tobias squeezes me tight.

MY BROTHER'S—WE'LL *see* turns into a—*we'll know*. Because once I get home, despite numerous text messages and calls on my part—ones that are blocked and eventually go to a line that's disconnected altogether when I try calling from my brother's phone—I never hear from Quentin again. In fact, Tobias and Xander never hear from him either. I don't see any news of him as a free agent, and I don't see him back on his team roster at their old college.

Quentin's disappeared like a ghost into the night. I'm half-worried that something terrible happened—something I'll never know about because my father can't let a grudge go.

Until New Year's Day when I'm at a friend's house, recovering from my hangover by sitting on the couch with fast food. My friend is watching college bowl games and I don't even know what teams are in them. I hadn't been interested in football this year. Nothing other than Tobias and Xander's games when I could catch them. Hating a football player as much as I hate Quentin will do that for you—ruin the whole damn sport.

So when I see him walk out on that field, playing for a different team, described as a top draft pick—I feel sick. When I see the girl who wraps her arms around his neck and kisses him when they win the game and raise the trophy surrounded by all the fans who have rushed down out of their seats—I feel like crying, but I don't. Instead, I make a silent promise to myself, that when the time comes, I'll ruin the name Undergrove.

GET Madison and Quentin's book RIVAL HEARTS.

ABOUT THE AUTHOR

Maggie Rawdon is a sports romance author living in the Midwest. She writes athletes with the kind of filthy mouths who will make you blush and swoon and the smart independent women who make them fall first. She has a weakness for writing frenemies whose fighting feels more like flirting and found families.

She loves real sports as much as the fictional kind and spends football season writing in front of the TV with her pups at her side. When she's not on editorial deadline you can find her bingeing epic historical dramas or fantasy series in between weekend hikes.

Join her newsletter here for sneak peeks and bonus content:
https://geni.us/MRBNews
Join her readers' group on FB here:
https://www.facebook.com/groups/rawdonsromanticrebels

    instagram.com/maggierawdonbooks
    tiktok.com/@maggierawdon
    facebook.com/maggierawdon

Made in United States
Cleveland, OH
22 June 2025